PROTECTING CLAIRE

CAPE Investigation

Book 3

Deanna L. Rowley

I'd like to thank my editor, Ann Attwood, for the wonderful job she does on my books.

CHAPTER ONE
CLAIRE

"Grandpa, what are you doing?" Claire Ambrose asked as she peeked over the front of his desk in his home office. She was only six years old, and she was standing as tall as she could, but the desk came up level with the bridge of her nose, so only her eyes and the top of her head showed.

Albert Ambrose smirked as he laid his pen down, folded his hands over his papers, bent down, and whispered, "Working."

Claire rolled her eyes and sighed heavily. "I know that, Grandpa, but what are you working on?" She made her way around the desk and climbed on his lap.

"I have decisions to make about work."

Claire frowned, then looked at him, and whispered, "Is it about the murder?"

Shocked, Albert reared back to demand, "What do you know about murder?"

"I read it."

"Where?"

Claire looked over both her shoulders, then pointed to the top of his desk. "There. I know I wasn't supposed to, but I was bored." She sighed heavily, enough that her bangs flew in the air, then looked at her grandfather, shook her finger at him, and said, "You should be ashamed of yourself."

"Me?" Her statement shocked Albert. "What did I do? You should be ashamed of yourself for reading things on my desk. Wait, you can read?"

"I'm not dumb, Grandpa." Claire rolled her eyes at him. "I even read two whole books on your shelves."

Albert shook his head and stared at his granddaughter. He knew she was smart, but he couldn't quite wrap his head around the fact that the only books on his shelves were dusty law books. Albert reserved the fiction and fun-to-read books for his library. Shaking his head again, he decided to address a different issue first. "Why should I be ashamed of myself?"

"My teacher would give you an 'N' for your penmanship."

"What's an 'N'?"

"Needs Improvement." Claire shook her head at him. He threw his head back and laughed.

"Sorry."

"You write like chicken scratches in the dirt. When I get bigger, I'm going to be a forever red-neck-tist, and I'll figure things out."

Albert laughed out right and asked, "What is a forever red-neck-tist?" He looked up at a movement in the doorway and motioned for his wife to enter. She carried a tray, holding a plate of cookies and two glasses of milk. Albert might be sixty years old, but he wasn't too old to have cookies and milk with their granddaughter.

"Thank you, dear," Albert said to his wife.

"So what are the two of you doing?" Sally asked as she passed them each a cookie, before taking one for herself, and sitting in the chair before his desk.

"Grandpa was about to tell me what murder was."

"What?" Sally asked, shocked.

"No, I wasn't," Albert said. He looked at his wife and rolled his eyes. "She told me she read the file on my desk and wanted to know about it." He refused to use the 'm' word around Claire.

"You do know she may be only six, but her reading level is that of someone double her age."

"Oh, no, I didn't. But, what I want to know is what a forever red-neck-tist is."

"A what?"

Albert repeated it, and the older couple shook their heads as they turned their attention to Claire. They had to wait, because she was in the process of dunking a cookie in her glass of milk. She sucked the milk off it, then took a big bite, before looking at her grandparents with a huge grin. "What?"

"Nothing." Albert grinned and handed her a napkin. "But what's the forever red-neck-tist thing?"

Claire rolled her eyes again, took another bite of her cookie, then leaned over the desk and fired up Albert's computer. She moved the mouse, clicked on several things, then pointed to the screen. "That." She went back to eating her cookies and milk, while Sally and Albert looked at the computer.

"You want to be a forensic scientist?"

"Yep, and I want to do something with handwriting. I forget what it's called. I saw it on TV once. It's cool."

"A handwriting analyst?" Sally hedged a guess.

"If that's what it's called." Claire shrugged, and she took a bite of her cookie. "So?" Claire asked, after she finished her cookies and milk. "What's murder?"

Albert sighed, and knew that no matter how much he put it off, she wouldn't let it rest until she got her answer.

"First off, murder is bad. It's when one person takes the life of another person."

"Is it like killing them?"

"Yes."

"Oh," she said, then shrugged her shoulders. "So, what do you have to do with it? Why is it your job to read about murder?"

"I'm a judge," Albert admitted. "It's my job to sit up on the bench and listen to everyone. The good guys and the bad, then a jury makes a decision on whether the bad person is good or bad."

"Okay, you listen, but why are you reading that?" She pointed to the file on his desk.

"Because, it's my job to weigh all the evidence and sentence the bad man. I have to think with my head and not my heart. Another person's life is in my hands, and I need to get it all right, before I put someone in jail."

"Ah, I understand." Claire patted his cheek and smiled. "I trust you know what you're doing."

"Thank you," Albert laughed, and Claire climbed down and ran away, yelling over her shoulder that she was going to go play now.

Shaking his head, he looked at his wife. "She never ceases to amaze me."

"I know," Sally giggled as she hugged him, and kissed the top of his head. "I'll leave you to your work. That's one thing I never liked about your job when you had to issue the sentence. I know how much it tears you up inside."

"Thanks, Sally." Albert kissed her cheek, and turned back to his work. When he was alone, he started reading all the evidence from the beginning. Hours later, when he cleaned up his office to head to the kitchen for dinner, he was happy with his decision. The defendant wouldn't be satisfied, but Albert would be able to sleep better with the man behind bars for the next twenty-five years. When he entered the kitchen, he went over and shook his son's hand, and kissed his daughter-in-law's cheek. They settled down to a nice meal, and talk centered around what everyone had done that day. Albert was grateful Claire didn't say anything about their conversation about murder.

*****

SIX MONTHS LATER

"What are you looking at?" The man with a three-inch scar across his left cheek glared at Claire. He shuddered when she continued to look at him. The worst part about the whole thing was the fact that she wasn't blinking.

"I'm studying your face, so when the police question me, I can give an accurate description of you."

"Ha, like that's going to happen. You're what? Five? They won't believe you."

"I'm six and a half, and they'll listen to me. I'll make sure of it." Claire wiggled her hands and sighed when the ropes holding her to the chair hadn't loosened in the last five minutes. Based on the sun outside of the house they were in, she had been held here for the previous six hours. When her stomach growled for the third time in as many minutes, she glared at him. "Are you going to add murder charges to your kidnapping charges?" she demanded of him.

"What did you say?" He stared at her in shock.

"Are you trying to kill me?"

"No, we're just holding you until we get what we want."

"Then, if you're not going to kill me, then feed me. I'm starving."

The man jumped to his feet and hurried out of the room. Once on the other side of the house, he kicked the foot of the man sleeping on the couch.

"Wake up, Rex."

"What?"

"Wake the fuck up. It's your turn to watch the brat," he said as he grabbed the bong on the table, and pulled a lighter from his pocket to light it. He kicked the other man's leg again, and barked out, "Call for a pizza, kid's hungry."

"Why me?"

"Because, she creeps me the fuck out." He drew the smoke into his lungs, and held it for several seconds before slowly releasing it, blowing smoke rings into the air. "You know what the brat asked me?" he asked as he passed the bong to the other man.

"What?" He coughed as he drew the smoke into his lungs.

"She asked if I was trying to murder her, because she's hungry."

"What the fuck, bro?"

"I know, but before that, she stared at me for so long, I could feel the hair in my beard grow."

"Why would she do that?"

"I asked the same thing. She said it was because she was studying my face to tell the police what I looked like when they questioned her. She wanted to get the details of my face down."

"What is she, five?" The second man snorted, and coughed as the smoke left his lungs.

"She said she was six and a half."

"Hey!" came a shout from the other room. "I'm not getting any younger here! Are you going to feed me, or what?"

"See," the first guy said as he pulled money from his pocket, and tossed it to the second guy. "Go, maybe it'll shut her up for a few minutes." He took a deep hit from the bong as the man left. Sitting on the couch and letting the pot fill his lungs, he felt himself relax for the first time since they had grabbed the girl on her way home from school.

Forty-five minutes later, there was pounding on the front door, and the man on the couch jerked awake, and hurried to look out the door, then opened it quickly. He stepped back, and the other guy came in carrying two pizza boxes and several plastic bags with white Styrofoam containers inside.

"Grab the bag from my arm. It's killing my wrist," the man said as he tried to get in the door with his arms full. It took several minutes, but the two were finally able to get in the door without dropping anything. They chuckled with their bumbling, and turned toward the kitchen, but screamed when they saw Claire standing there.

"How the hell did you get loose?" they demanded.

"You don't know how to tie knots tight. What's for supper?" she asked, and walked up to them, and took a box from the man. She carried it to the kitchen. The men followed her and watched as she pulled up a chair, opened the box, and grabbed a slice of pizza. The three of them settled in to eat, and after everyone finished one piece, she looked at them and asked. "Do you guys have good lawyers?"

"Why do we need a lawyer?"

"Because, you're going to be arrested for kidnapping me." She took a bite of her second slice of pizza and studied them. "Why did you kidnap me anyway?"

"Your grandfather put our friend in jail. We're only keeping you until we get our friend out of jail. When we get him, we'll call him and give him your location." They continued to eat, and he said, "We're not going to hurt you. We just want your grandpa to know that we mean business."

Claire rolled her eyes and shook her head. "You know it doesn't work that way. Not only can I give them both your descriptions, but your fingerprints are all over this house." She continued to eat as the two stared at her. "Oh, and don't forget, along with the kidnapping charges, there are the drug charges, and maybe they will charge you for extortion. I'm not sure about that one. I haven't read that far yet."

They continued to stare at her, then they chuckled and shook their heads. "You are shitting us. You don't know all that about the law. You're making it up from watching TV."

"Whatever," Claire shrugged, but she suddenly dropped her pizza on her plate, jumped to her feet, then dropped to the floor, and crawled beneath the table. Before either of the men could react, the front door was kicked open, and yelling preceded the police and FBI storming the house from the front and back.

"POLICE! FREEZE!"

"FBI! FREEZE!" The authorities had the two men cuffed and walked out the door in less than three minutes after breaching the house.

Claire crawled out from beneath the table, with her arms crossed around her chest. She tapped her foot, and asked, "What took you so long? I've been missing for almost seven hours."

The police officers stared at her and looked around at each other. "You're not scared?" one of them asked.

"Why would I be scared? They were idiots. Couldn't stop getting high long enough to really do anything. No, I'm not hurt." She reached for another slice of pizza and grabbed her backpack from the back of a chair. "Let's go, it's getting late, and I have homework to do." She strode through the house with her head held high. Outside, she stood on the front porch and saw the two men sitting in a cop car. She went over and asked the officer to open the window.

"Sorry about your luck. Maybe when you're sitting in jail you'll think about what you did. Your biggest mistake was doing drugs. Didn't you know they fry your brain cells? Maybe if you didn't do them, your plan would have worked." She turned and walked away.

One of the men in the back of the squad car turned to the police officer, and said, "Please, get us out of here. We'll confess to everything, just get us away from her. She's creepy."

The officer chuckled, and after talking to his co-workers, he climbed in the car and drove away.

CHAPTER TWO
MAX

Thirteen-year-old Max Abbott looked at his best friend, and said, "I'm going first."

"No way," Sebastian Patrick O'Grady said. "It was my idea."

"And who got all the supplies?"

"Fine... rock, paper, scissors." Bas held out his fisted hand, and moved it up and down.

"Best two out of three," Max said, as he pumped his hand.

"Deal."

They counted to three, and Max laughed. "Ha, scissors cut paper. I win."

"That hand, but we still have two to go," Bas groused, and they pumped fists again.

"Even," they said as one when they both did rock. The next hand, Max won again with his scissors against Bas's paper.

"That was two out of three!" Max crowed.

"The second one didn't count. It was even." They did it again, and Max still won.

"Fine." Dejected at his loss, Bas watched as his best friend picked up his bicycle, and wheeled it over to the spot they had designated as the starting point.

"Be sure to maintain your speed. Don't chicken out as you approach the ramp. Don't coast going down the hill. Pump your legs the whole time. We need to see how far in the air you can fly." Bas laughed at his friend's grin.

"I know, I can't wait. When I'm done, you can go next."

"Let's see how things work with you, then we can tweak the ramp if we need to." Bas started running down the hill, but Max called him back.

"Bas!"

"What?" Bas huffed when he returned.

Max held out his fisted hand and grinned. "See you on the other side." They fist-bumped, and Max waited at the top of the hill, until Bas reached the pre-determined destination. Max watched as Bas picked up the video camera they'd taken from Sebastian's house, and after giving the thumbs-up sign to Max, Bas settled down on the ground, and pointed the camera at Max.

Taking a deep breath, Max closed his eyes, calming his nerves. Opening his eyes, he focused on the mouth of the ramp he was aiming for. Feeling invincible, Max grinned as he started pumping his legs as fast as they could go. After only a few feet, he had to squint, because the air rushing in his face caused his eyes to water, but he never took his eyes off the ramp entrance. Everything around him was a blur, and as he hit his target, he heard Bas yell encouragement. Max continued to pump his legs until he was airborne, then he let out a loud whoop of joy, threw his hands in the air, and kicked out his legs. He was so high, he thought he was taller than the trees. When the bike started to descend, Max put his hands on the handlebars, but he was only able to get one foot on a pedal before the ground rushed up toward him.

Wanting to slow his speed, he stuck out the foot that wasn't on a pedal and screamed in both horror and pain at the impact. The next thing he knew, Bas was leaning over him, with tears streaming down his face.

"*Max! Max!* Are you okay? Max, talk to me, Max!

"Why are you crying?"

"Max!" Bas screamed, and threw himself on his best friend.

"Ow!" Max yelled, and tried to push his friend off him. "What happened?"

"You crashed and burned. Don't move. I mean it, Max. I have to go call for an ambulance. Trust me," Bas said. "Here." Bas shoved the video camera in Max's hands and said, "Do not move. Watch the tape, and you'll understand. I don't want you to have a back or neck injury, but I have to call the police. Your foot is messed up. I'll be back, I promise." Bas left, leaving Max all alone on the mountain road. It was good, because this road was barely traveled, which was terrible, because no one would be coming and find Max lying in the middle of the road.

Max must have passed out, because the next thing he knew, Bas was talking to him. He screamed in pain at whatever was being done to his leg, and passed out again. The next time he came to, two men were working on him.

"What's going on?" he asked weakly. "Who are you?"

"We're the EMTs. Your friend called us," one man said as he smirked at Max. "So, how was the ride?" He looked over his shoulder, and Max could only assume it was at the ramp he and Bas had made.

"Great, but I think the landing was what killed me."

"Naw." The other EMT grinned. "You're not dead, but you're banged up pretty bad. You won't be riding your bike for some time. Not only did you break your ankle, but your friend here took your bike apart."

"What! Why the hell would he do that?" Max demanded, then screamed when he was rolled over, and a rigid board was slid beneath him, then he was lifted. When he looked down and saw the back wheel of his bike actually embedded in his foot, he passed out again. The last thing he heard was Bas telling him he would call his parents to meet him at the hospital.

*****

MAX SLOWLY OPENED HIS eyes and tried to swallow, but his mouth was so dry, it felt like his tongue was stuck to the roof. When he felt something at his lips, he sucked and sighed in relief. That happened several times, before he finally woke enough to look around.

"Where am I?" he croaked out, and immediately saw Bas's face above his.

"You're awake."

"Yeah, what happened?"

"You crash-landed after you flew off the ramp."

"Yeah." Max grinned. "I remember thinking I was taller than the trees. It was great. But, why am I here? This is a hospital, right?"

"It is," Bas said, then pulled up a chair and opened the six-inch viewing screen on the video recorder. The two boys watched as Max came flying down the hill, up the ramp, and passed through the air. Both of them screamed in excitement.

As Max fell, they watched him put his foot down, then he buckled into himself, and went ass over tea kettle.

"Holy shit, so what happened?" Max looked at his best friend in wide-eyed shock. "I didn't feel a thing."

"I showed this to the doctor, and he believes the force of your impact was all on that one foot. It snapped, then with the momentum of the speed you were going, that caused you to tumble end over end. You ended up about a hundred feet away. You're pretty banged up." Bas sat back in his chair, and wouldn't look at Max as he put the recorder away.

"Bas, don't hold anything back now. We've been best friends all our lives, so don't be a chicken shit now."

"It's all my fault. It was my idea to build a ramp in the first place."

"So, that doesn't mean shit. We did this together. Tell me what's wrong with me." Before Bas could answer, the door opened, and Max's parents strode in. Max sighed in relief, then tried to push his mother away when she started kissing his face.

"Mom, eww."

"Glad your awake, Son." Max's father nodded at him. Max noticed he didn't touch him. This was odd, because his father always patted his shoulder or back whenever he was close. He had started doing that ever since Max told him he was too old for hugs anymore, but right about now, that was all Max wanted—a hug.

"I was trying to get Bas to tell me what's wrong, but he won't say anything."

"That's because we told him not to," Kurt Abbott said. He sat on the end of Max's bed and laid a hand on his son's knee. Looking at him, he sighed, then began. "We saw the video of what happened. Your mother and I discussed it, and we won't punish you for doing something so stupid."

"Why?" It shocked Max to hear he wouldn't be punished.

"Because your injuries are punishment enough," Elena, Max's mother, said. "First, you'll use a wheelchair."

"For the rest of my life?" Max stared at his parents in shock.

"No," Kurt said. "Okay, let's start from your head and work our way down. As I tell you of your injuries, just be lucky you survived. You have a concussion. You've been out of it for the last week. You have black eyes and road rash on your cheeks. Your neck and spine are okay—no damage there, or to your internal organs, but your collarbone is broken, along with your left ankle. You actually shattered the ankle, and right now, you have several plates and screws to hold it together. The wheelchair is so no weight will be put on the foot or the collarbone."

"How will I get around then? I can't just sit on my behind and do nothing."

"There's where I come in." Bas perked up with a wide grin on his face. "Since it's summer vacation, I can be at your house every day."

"With supervision," Elena said firmly. "I know you're thirteen, and legally you can stay home by yourself, but because of your actions, you can't be trusted not to do something stupid again. Your father convinced me to allow Bas to come over. If I had my way, he'd be banned from the house, but I can't do that to both of you. When you leave here, Mrs. Cromwell will be coming to the house every day to keep an eye on both of you boys."

When it looked like Bas was going to object, Kurt interjected, "It's that, or you don't come over, Bas. Take it or leave it."

"Take it," both boys answered together.

"When can I get out of here?" Max asked.

"Now that you're awake, it should be a couple of days. You still have several tests to go through."

"Oh," Elena said as she studied both boys, with what they would later describe as an evil grin. "I've taken the liberty to discuss this with Oliver and Marie."

"My parents?" Bas asked in shock, looking at Max, and they both groaned. "What did you discuss?"

"Marie and I have gone to the school and talked to the principal. Though it's summer vacation, he mentioned that you were both struggling in English class this year. You passed by the skin of your teeth, so with that said, we've got a list of books from the school. Each week for the next twelve weeks, you will read one book and write a thousand-word report on that book."

"And if we don't?" Max frowned at his mother.

"If you don't, then for each week you fail to do the assignment, then that is two weeks you boys can't be together."

"However," Kurt took up the conversation. "The book reports need to be totally different from one another, and you can count on the four of us adults critiquing your work."

"Can we read the same book at the same time?" Max asked.

"Yes, but..." Kurt paused for effect "...you have to have different reports. Both your mother and I have read your past work, as has Bas's parents. We even went so far as to exchange your work. They know how you write, and we know how Bas writes. This will help us with reading your reports."

"How long do we have?"

"You will start a book Monday morning. It doesn't matter what the book is. When you get home, you and Bas can go through the list your mother got and decide... and boys," Kurt said sternly, as he glared at them. "No deviating from the list. The reports are due by 6 p.m. on Friday evening. We parents will read them and discuss them together on Sunday afternoons. We've already agreed to have a cookout every Sunday until further notice."

"I suggest you go through the list before Max is released from the hospital," Elena said as she opened her purse, and pulled out two folded pieces of paper. She passed one to each boy. "Use the back of that paper to make a list of your reading order. One of us will make sure you each have the next book by Monday."

The boys took the list, but didn't look at them until after the doctor, nurse, and Max's parents stepped out.

"Holy shit," Bas said as he looked at this list. "These are old people's books."

Max looked at the list, and groaned, *"Gone with the Wind? To Kill a Mockingbird? Wuthering Heights? Grapes of Wraps?"*

"Wrath. Not wrap, wrath." Bas grinned at him.

"Fine, whatever. Are we really going to do this?"

"Might as well. I don't know if I can go the whole summer without seeing you."

"I know. I might be laid up, but we can still hang out." Max stared at the list, lay back on his pillows, and sighed heavily. "Let's hope it's a shitty summer, and we don't miss out on anything, because of the weather. I can be stuck in the house reading if it's raining, but not if it's hot and sunny. That would kill me."

"I know," Bas sighed as they studied the list of books, and came up with a plan of attack. Little did they know that summer would be a turning point in their friendship and their lives.

CHAPTER THREE
SEBASTIAN

"You ready?" Sebastian Patrick O'Grady asked his best friend Max Abbott as he stood behind his wheelchair to push him to the dining room, where both their parents were getting Sunday dinner ready. This was the first week they would get their reviews back from the book reports they had been forced to write if they wanted to continue to hang out.

Maybe making the ramp and using it had been a stupid idea at the time, but just in the last two weeks, the boys had grown closer. Mrs. Cromwell, the babysitter, was there at seven every morning. Bas arrived by eight. It had helped reading with the rain that had come down all week. It was now the weekend, and they might be able to dodge the raindrops long enough to have a cookout. All week had been gray, cloudy, and dismal. Today it was bright and sunny. With a jump in his step, Bas pushed Max out of his room and down the hall.

Bas's family called him Pat, after his middle name of Patrick. He had an old family tradition that all the firstborn men in the family would have the first name of Sebastian, but because there were four generations of Sebastian O'Grady's still alive and kicking, everyone except for the oldest went by their middle name, but Bas went by two. His family called him Pat, and his best friend and friends at school called him Bas—short for Sebastian. He was unsure what he preferred, so he shrugged it off and answered to both.

At the entrance to the patio, Bas called out, "Dad!" and watched as both Oliver O'Grady and Kurt Abbott turned to look. They laughed as they looked at each other, then over to the boys.

"Oops," Kurt said as he and Oliver started forward. Together they gripped the sides of the wheelchair and brought it down the two steps to the deck.

"Thanks," both boys said, and Bas wheeled Max over to his usual spot at the table. After situating his best friend, he turned to his mother. "Do you need any help?"

"No, we're almost ready. Did you wash your hands?"

"Oops," Bas said as he headed back to the house.

"Young man?" he heard over his shoulder as Max's mother asked him.

"Yep, did it before leaving my room."

Bas hurried back to Max's room and used the bathroom, then washed his hands. The room was like his own. He was in it so much. As he stepped out of the bathroom, he smiled at the pile of pillows they had set up as their "reading" spot. At first it had been hard, but once Bas got into the book, he couldn't seem to put it down. They had set up a schedule that they would read for so long, take a break, read some more, then stop for the day at three in the afternoon—the time a regular school day stopped. Including lunch, they only took three breaks from nine to three. It was only the first week, but Bas liked it so far.

Back outside, he stopped and grabbed the package of napkins his mother hollered in for him to get, and joined everyone on the deck. Taking his seat to Max's right, he looked at the table and grinned. His father had just put a gigantic plate of ribs in the center of the table and Kurt, Max's dad, put down a plate of corn on the cob. There had to be at least three dozen ears there. He rubbed his stomach and had to wait until grace was said, then he fixed Max's plate before filling his own. He'd learned that Max could eat, but couldn't hold a heavy dish, because of the sling for his broken collarbone.

The two worked together without any words, and at one point, Bas looked up and frowned at the adults. "What?"

They shook their heads, and all said, "Nothing." Bas shook his head and continued to fill both plates. Once he finished, they looked at each other, grinned, and picked up their first ear of corn, not only of the day, but of the season.

By silent agreement, they began eating it, and two seconds in, it turned into a contest. They didn't come up for air until the cob was clean.

"I won!" Max crowed, then laughed as corn fell out of his mouth.

"Boys," both Elena and Marie said. The boys looked at their mothers and grinned with mouths ringed with butter and small pieces of corn dripping off their lips and chins. The adults shook their heads, and breathed a sigh of relief when the rest of the meal progressed with no more eating contests.

It wasn't until the dishes had been cleared, the fruit brought out for dessert, and the adults had a cup of coffee, that the conversation turned.

"Well, boys," Oliver began. "We read your book reports."

Bas looked at Max, and knew the fear he saw in his friend's eyes was mirrored in his own.

"And?" Bas asked.

"And," Oliver drew out the word and looked at the other adults, before turning his attention back to the two boys. "We're surprisingly impressed."

The adults laughed, then the boys both released a heavy sigh.

"We could tell that the two of you read the book by the points you made in your reports. But, what really impressed us was the fact that each of you had a different point of view. Separately, they are great papers, but together, it's like they make up a whole. It's hard to explain. It's almost like your minds are in sync with each other. Keep up the good work."

Bas looked at Max and beamed. They had agreed to read this first book silently, then write the report. It had been Bas's suggestion to wait until the end of the summer and exchange the pieces, so they could read each other's work.

"However," Elena Abbott spoke. "You won't get the book reports back."

"What? Why?" Bas asked. "Max and I were going to wait until the end of the summer and read each other's work."

"Okay, we can do that, but after you read each other's work, you'll give them back to us."

"Why?" Max asked.

"Because, we don't want you to cheat and turn them in if you are assigned to read those books in class. It wouldn't be fair to the other students," Maria, Bas's mother, said. None of the adults told them the book list was for freshman-level college students.

"Oh," both boys said, dejected. "But we can read them? Right?"

"You can."

They nodded, and Max helped as much as he could to clean up, but he couldn't do much with his injuries. With the adult males' help, he was put back in the house, and the two boys went to Max's room to hang out. When Maria and Elena found them hours later, they were both snuggled into their reading places with the next book.

The rest of the summer turned out the way the first week had been. The whole time it seemed to rain during the week, and the only good day had been on Sundays when the two families met for a cookout. Once the sling came off, Max was able to wheel himself in his chair. During their break from reading, they had used the time to practice going in and out of the house with the wheelchair. Max had been able to get a running start and hop his wheelchair out the door. Laughing, Bas stood several feet away to slow him down, so he didn't go off the end of the deck. When their parents saw what they had accomplished, their only reaction was to shake their heads.

Bas stayed home for three days straight one week and didn't contact Max the whole time. He had to go out of town with his parents to visit his aunts and uncles. He had been so bored that he had found a quiet corner and read that week's current book. When his cousins picked on him, he ignored them. And that was only the first few hours after arriving. Later that night, Bas found himself set up in his cousin's room and groaned when he realized it was his cousin, Dwight, the bookworm cousin.

Bas kept to himself and hovered beneath the blankets with a flashlight to read. Hours later, he heard a strange sound. After he whipped the blanket off his head, he looked at Dwight, and demanded. "What's that sound?"

"Internet connection."

"What's that?" Bas asked as he climbed out of bed, and went over to where his cousin was sitting at his desk. "What's that?" Bas pointed to the machine sitting in the middle of the desk.

"This is a computer, and I'm dialing up to get a signal on the internet," Dwight said, and proceeded to answer all of Bas's questions.

"This is the future, man," Dwight said at one point. Once the weird noises stopped, he showed Bas how to look for things on the worldwide web. They spent the whole visit in Dwight's room. On the way home, Bas talked non-stop to his parents about what he had discovered on the internet, and what it was, what it could do, and told them he wanted to get a job to buy one. He didn't see his parents exchange looks. Even though he was an only child, he never begged for overpriced ticket items. If he wanted something, he'd come up with a way to get the money. One winter, he went around and shoveled people's walks or driveways. Another summer, he mowed people's lawns. He couldn't wait to get home to talk to Max about what he had discovered. Together, they would come up with something to do to make money.

Bas worked out a plan for both him and Max to make some money to buy a computer. By the time Max was ready to do the work, he had healed, had his cast removed, and gone through physical therapy. When Bas arrived one day, he was shocked that Max opened the door with no chair or crutches.

"You're healed?"

"Yep, how are you?"

"Good," Bas said as he walked in, and stopped in his tracks. "Whoa."

"What?"

"You grew." Bas pointed at him with a frown.

"No, I didn't."

"Yes, you did. We were the same height before your accident. Now, look at you." Bas stepped right up to him and looked Max directly in the nose. Before, they were eye to eye.

"Oh," Max said as his cheeks turned pink. "So, what are we doing today? We've read all the books, done all the reports. School starts next week. What do you want to do before it starts?"

"I thought we could start a leaf-raking business."

"Why would we want to do that?"

"Because, if we do something stupid again, I'll never get to see you. Your mother will lock you in the attic until you're twenty-one. You're my best friend. I don't need to lose you now." Bas moved his head to the side, then smirked. "Though, I probably could rig something up and climb up the side of the house to reach you."

"You ass," Max laughed as he pushed his best friend. "We don't have an attic."

"Okay, then the basement. I'm sure I can dig a tunnel."

Laughing, they went to the kitchen to look for something to eat. It seemed like they were both hungry all the time. This was Mrs. Cromwell's last day, and it surprised Bas to walk in and see a massive breakfast of pancakes, bacon, scrambled eggs, juice, and milk waiting for the two of them. In less than thirty minutes, it was gone.

"What are you boys going to do today?" Mrs. Cromwell asked as she sipped her tea, and watched as the boys cleared the table.

"I'm going to talk to Max about starting a leaf raking business. I want to save money to get a computer for Christmas," Bas paused in cleaning up to tell her.

"I'm going to talk to Bas about signing up for soccer next week when school starts."

"We can't do sports, school, *and* business."

"Sure you can," Mrs. Cromwell said. "It's all in the planning. Monday to Friday, you do school and sports. You can do your homework every night. Come the weekend, do the leaf raking business. If you have the right tools, you can do a lot during the weekend. I'll even be your first customer."

"You'd do that for us?" Bas asked. He looked at Max. "What do you think? Can we do it?"

"Hey, if we can read *Grapes of Wrath*, *War and Peace*, and *Gone with the Wind*, and understand them, we can do anything." They high-fived each other, and left to go to Max's room to plan.

The next day was Saturday, and Bas showed up at Max's house early. "What's up?" Max asked.

"Mrs. Cromwell called me and asked me to get you to come over to her house by eight."

"Oh," Max said, then went and told his parents what he was doing. Together they went out, and because Max hadn't replaced his bike yet, they walked the mile to her house. They lived in the Rockies in northern Idaho, roughly about thirty miles south of the Canadian border. Usually, snow hit before the leaves were even off the trees, but this year had been a weird weather year. It was like God had saved the sunshine for when the boys were out and about. It was now almost the end of August, and the weather finally decided to cooperate.

They arrived at Mrs. Cromwell's and weren't surprised when she was waiting on the front porch for them. She strolled down the steps and directed them around the house to the garage. After she opened the doors, she stood back, and said, "I have a proposition for you. I lost my husband three years ago, and my children all live in a different states. If you do my leaves and clean the snow off my driveway, my sidewalk, and porch steps, I'll allow you to use this equipment." She stepped inside and turned on a light.

"What's that?" Bas pointed to the pile of objects in the center of one garage bay.

"There are rakes, shovels, two leaf blowers, but only one snowblower. It's a walk-behind and has the protective shroud around it."

"You'll let us use this stuff? For other people?"

"Yes, Sebastian. But, only on the condition that you do my home first." She pulled a keyring from her pocket and handed it to them. "This is the key to the garage. I'm not always home, but I like to come home to a clean drive. I'm getting up in years and don't really have the energy to do it myself." She crooked her finger to have them follow her. Out the back of the garage she walked into her back yard. "As you can see, the leaves are already beginning to fall. I have a feeling we're going to have a hard, cold, brutal winter. If you could, I'd like all the leaves mulched and swept and then blown onto my flower beds."

Bas looked over at her and frowned. "How do we mulch and sweep the leaves?"

"Oh," Mrs. Cromwell laughed. "Come here." They went back into the garage, and she pointed to the riding lawnmower. "You cut the grass, like usual. Then you drive around in circles to blow the leaves in a row. This is a sweeper. You drive around with it behind the mower, and it sweeps the leaves up. Then you can use the leaf blowers to move them to where you want them to go." Mrs. Cromwell actually waved them aside and demonstrated how to do it. The boys laughed and spent the rest of the morning cleaning up all the leaves that had fallen from the trees. They promised they'd be back the next day to get the equipment. On the way back to Max's house, the two boys discussed what they could do with that equipment. Instead of rushing straight home, they stopped at all the places along the way where they knew a single elderly person lived, or an elderly couple. By the time they reached Max's home, they had twenty-five customers on their list.

For the next four and a half months, the boys were extremely busy. It turned out that Bas was the mastermind of the business. While Max was the brawn. They both did the work, but with Bas's business sense, by the time Christmas came, they had enough money to both buy a computer, as well as a new bike for Max. However, they were too tired to do anything with it. They had started their leaf business, which had morphed into a snow plowing business in no time. At first, it was hard to manage their time with work, school, and sports, but after two weeks of fumbling, they got into a routine.

Two weeks before Christmas, the boys' parents met for dinner, leaving the boys home at Max's house to do homework. It was a Friday night, and who did homework on a Friday night? Especially, two fourteen-year-old boys, and it was the beginning of their Christmas break. They would be off for the next two weeks. When asked, both boys said they wanted to get it done and out of the way.

"Thanks for coming," Kurt said as he stood when the O'Grady's arrived. They all settled down, and Oliver asked.

"So what's up?"

"I'm going to get right to the point. Six months ago, Max's accident scared me shitless. Oh, I knew he survived and that he would walk again, no, my fear was that once he healed, they'd do it all over again."

"Yeah, me too," Oliver sighed. "But, I feared Pat would be the next one in the hospital."

"I know, but now..." Kurt shook his head and actually reached up and wiped a tear from the corner of his eye. "Now, look at them. Home on a Friday night doing homework when they have two weeks to do it. They've not only done one business, but two, all while going to school and participating in sports, and not as bench warmers. They've started every soccer game and every basketball game. I don't know about you Oliver, Marie, but I'm dammed proud of my boy."

"Me too," Oliver said as he placed his drink order with the waitress, then one for his wife. They quickly ordered appetizers and their meal. "I want to do something to show how proud of them I am, but I don't know what."

"That's why we invited you to dinner," Elena spoke. "The boys started the leaf business, because Bas saw a computer at his cousin's house. He told Max all about it. Now, this year, they have them in the school, and they are both taking classes to learn how to use them."

"Okay," Oliver frowned. "What are you saying?"

"I'm saying that Kurt and I are going over to that new computer store after dinner to buy Max his first computer for Christmas. I think they've been so busy that they forgot all about it," she admitted, then giggled.

"What?"

"Max comes home exhausted every night. When I do his laundry, I empty his pockets. One day I pulled out almost a hundred dollars in cash. I asked him where it came from, and all he said was tips. I have a jar in the laundry room that I throw the money from his pants in." She paused, looked around the table, and leaned in. "I'm on the third jar. It's like he's forgotten about it. Kurt took the first two jars to the bank and opened an account in his name."

"Wow, I never thought of that," Marie said. "I put it in an envelope and hand it to Pat." She frowned. "Makes me wonder how many envelopes are in his room." She giggled. "I'll wash his clothes, but I refuse to clean his room. I love my son with all my heart, but a fourteen-year-old boy's room. No." The adults shared a laugh and enjoyed their meal together. It turned out that both sets of parents went to the computer store and talked to the salesman for a long time before making their purchases.

It was Oliver that said as they waited to be rung up. "I wonder how their homework will be now that they can type it up, then print it out."

Christmas morning in both homes were put on hold until both Bas and Max made their rounds of cleaning off sidewalks and snow blowing driveways. By the time they returned home, both their arms were loaded with presents from their customers, sweets to share with their family, and wads of money stuffed in their pockets.

Later that afternoon, they met again and talked about their gifts. They found out they had both received the exact same computer, and because of their computer classes at school, they had been able to set up an e-mail account, so they could talk whenever they wanted. By the time they returned to school in the New Year, both boys were over six foot, had developed muscles, started to grow hair on their faces, and their voices had deepened. The girls were all over them when they returned, but they kept to their grueling schedule until the spring when there was no snow to shovel and no leaves falling. With a new season, it brought new adventures to the boys. They had discovered that girls weren't as bad as they thought.

CHAPTER FOUR
CLAIRE

Sixteen-year-old Claire Ambrose strode into her grandfather's home office and stood just inside the door. She looked at the man sitting behind his desk, and demanded, "Are you allowed to be out of bed?"

"I'm not dead yet, little miss. I refuse to lie in bed and let the Grim Reaper take me. If I'm going out, I'm going out doing what I love."

"Oh," Claire said and exhaled. "Sorry, I yelled at you, but you've been so sick lately."

"I know, but I felt better today. What brings you here?"

"I heard Mom and Dad talking about you giving the nurse a hard time. I thought I'd come give it back to you."

Albert Ambrose laughed and held out his arms to his only grandchild. She ran to him, crawled on his lap, and hugged him, the same thing she had done for years. After a long time of silence, Claire sat up, inhaled a deep breath, then let it out in a rush.

"Why the heavy sigh?"

"I need to ask you something, but I don't know how to ask without upsetting you. It's been on my mind for a long, long time."

"That long, huh?" He squeezed her, then pointed to the chair in front of his desk. He studied the woman before him and shook his head. While Claire was only sixteen, she was currently a sophomore in college. They had her tested in the first grade and found she had an outrageously high IQ, and she had flown through high school. Now at the age of sixteen, she was going to the local university, but she was taking two different majors. Albert knew that by the time Claire graduated, she would have two PhDs. One would be in Forensic Science, the other would be in Forensic Psychology. The last time they spoke, two weeks ago, she talked about getting more degrees in Criminal Psychology, and she'd already received her Master's in Document Analysis. He shook his head at just how smart she was.

"So, what did you want to ask me?"

"You have to promise not to get upset." Claire jumped to her feet and took the tea tray from the housekeeper, and proceeded to pour them both a cup before she settled back in her seat. With her cup of tea cradled in her hands, she looked at her grandfather with a raised brow. "Promise you won't get upset, and I want the truth, and nothing but the truth."

Albert laughed, until he began coughing. He waved off Claire's concerns. After settling back in his chair, he sipped his own tea and looked at her. "I promise."

"Okay, remember ten years ago when I was kidnapped? How did you find me?"

"Oh, that." Albert waved it off like it was nothing, but seeing the look on her face, he settled further into his chair. "You know that I was a federal judge, right?"

"Yes, before that, you sat on the local bench for a long time. Weren't you the youngest man to be appointed judge in our state?"

"Yes, and with the title of judge, comes the hassle." He held up his hand as he spoke. "You wanted total honesty. Back then, I thought it was best to keep you in the dark, but since I'm dying and don't have long to live, it's time you knew the truth."

"Really?"

"Yes, against your parents' wishes, I'll tell you what happened." He sipped his tea and watched as Claire stood, folded her legs beneath her, and settled back down. "When I was appointed judge, it took about six months before the threatening letters started to arrive." At Claire's frown, Albert elaborated, "Death threats against my family and me, but no names were ever mentioned. It was always quote your family unquote. At first, I didn't take them seriously, not until my clerk saw the third one. He called the police, and I had to admit I had thrown the other two out. They were not happy with me."

"Can you tell me who sent the threats?"

"People I put away in prison, or their family members. They thought if they could threaten my family and me, I'd somehow reduce their sentences."

"Is that why it took you longer to issue a sentence than any other judge?"

"Yes, to me, it's not only a legal decision, it's a moral one. And sometimes, it's an emotional one. I know I shouldn't let my emotions in, but sometimes it's hard not to."

"You wouldn't be human if you didn't. What about the people that kidnapped me?" Claire looked at her grandfather and smirked. "They were kind of idiots, you know?"

"Yeah, I do." They shared a chuckle. She had told him everything that had happened, which was when she was tested for her IQ. That was when the family found out Claire Ambrose had a photographic memory, as well as a high IQ. All that happened right after her kidnapping and Claire had forgotten about it, until she realized that her grandfather wouldn't be alive for much longer. She knew she would get answers from him faster than going to her parents. They wanted to keep her bundled in bubble wrap. Well, at least her mother did. Her father, Timothy, would try to keep Mindy, Claire's mother, out of her hair. It was bad enough to hire a bodyguard and actually paid for them to get an education right along with Claire. But, since she was only sixteen she couldn't say or do anything about it. She'd bide her time until she was a legal adult, then cut the apron strings herself.

"So, how did you find me? Because I know you were behind my rescue."

"I was. But, don't be too hard on your parents. They had no clue what I had done when you were born. So, it was up to me to take matters into my own hands."

"Why?"

"When Mindy was pregnant with you, I became a judge. It wasn't until after I was sworn in and pictures were taken by the media, and I received my first death threat that I realized my mistake. Your picture was forever connected with me, not that I didn't mind. You were a beautiful baby, and are an even more beautiful young woman right now. But, after my clerk took the threats seriously, I reached out to a former buddy of mine."

"May I ask why he's former?"

"Because, we went to college together and lost touch with each other over the years. Nothing sinister happened, unless you call that thing called life sinister. He lived half a country away over on the east coast, whereas we're landlocked here in Nebraska."

"Okay." Claire grinned and sipped her tea. "So, why did you reach out to him?"

"He was an FBI agent. Since then, he retired, and I heard that he passed away last year. Anyway, I contacted him and told him about the threats against my family and me. He showed up on my doorstep three weeks later. Said he had something that would make me sleep at night."

"What was that?"

"He had a tracking device. You were a baby. He happened to arrive at the time your grandmother and I took you to have your shots. You know how much your mother freaked out when you cried. She wasn't okay with the first set when you were six weeks old. She ended up crying harder than you. That's why your grandmother and I volunteered to take you. Anyway, my friend offered to go with us. He was in the room with us, and after both nurses gave you a shot in each leg, he told us to turn around. We did. Your grandmother knew what was going on."

"What was going on?" Claire asked as she leaned forward and placed her empty cup on her grandfather's desk. Claire smirked when he only raised a brow at the coasters sitting beside the cup. Albert refused to say anything until Claire put the cup on a coaster.

"My friend said he had a tracking device. It was something new the agency was trying, to keep track of their undercover operatives. Very cloak and dagger, spy stuff."

"Okay. But, what does that have to do with me?"

"He injected one of those tracking devices in you. I have no idea where. I didn't see where it went in. It could be in your leg, arm, butt, or even your stomach or neck. The only way to know for sure would be to get a full-body x-ray to see if you can find it."

Claire sat there for several minutes in stunned silence. "Wow, I don't know if I want to be pissed, freaked, or cool about it. It's a lot to take in."

"It is, and I'm sorry if you're not cool with it, but at the time, that was the only way I could think to keep you safe." Albert slowly rose to his feet, shuffled his walker in front of him, and went to the other side of the room. He pulled a painting toward him to reveal a wall safe. After opening it, he reached in, withdrew a small envelope and brought it back to Claire, but not before shutting the safe and replacing the framed picture. After he settled back in his chair, he leaned up and handed the envelope to Claire.

"What's this?" she asked as she took it from him.

"That's the information on your chip. You're old enough and have that photographic memory that you can have this now. When I found out you had been taken, I called my buddy and told him what had happened. It took him some time to get the correct information. He had a lot of explaining to do. He hadn't asked permission to use the chip."

"Holy cow, Grandpa, are you saying I have stolen government equipment embedded inside my body somewhere?"

"Yep."

"Okay, now it's cool." They shared a laugh. "After I told my friend what had happened, he found the correct information and called it into the local field office. He told them about your kidnapping and threats against me. They blew it off at first, until the locals called in a kidnapping. They took it seriously then. In a little over two hours after the locals called the Feds, they were kicking down the door to the house you were in."

"What exactly does this do?" Claire asked as she held up the envelope, without even opening it.

"That is a list of numbers. When they are entered into the computer, as they are written, they will immediately locate you. It's so accurate that there is only a three-foot variance." He held out his hand for the envelope, then called her around the desk, and Claire watched as he typed the numbers.

"You don't have to put them into any program?"

"Yes, but I already had the program on my computer."

"Grandpa, are you keeping tabs on me when I'm at school?"

"I don't know what you're talking about," he deadpanned, then grinned. "All the information you need is in that envelope." He pointed to the screen and moved the mouse when a blinking red dot appeared. Claire watched, and the green surrounding the dot became clearer, and more precise, until she was looking down on her grandfather's house.

"Oh, wow. That's awesome."

"It is. I want you to take the information in that envelope and commit it to memory. If you ever find someone you trust, I want you to give them that information. If anything happens to you, then they'll have the ability to find you." Albert paused and studied his granddaughter. "That is unless you have it removed."

"No way, I think it's cool, and I like the idea of the cavalry coming to the rescue if something happens." Claire wrapped her arms around her frail grandfather, and kissed his cheek. "I love you, Grandpa. Thank you for loving me enough to protect me from the evils of this world."

"That's why I did it. Because, I love you. With you wanting to get into the forensics side of law enforcement, I know you'll be surrounded by scientists and police officers alike, but I like the idea of just a little bit of added security. It makes me sleep better at night."

"Thanks, Grandpa. I love you." Claire kissed his cheek again, and rested her head against the top of his.

*****

THE NEXT DAY, CLAIRE woke to someone screaming in her house. She ran from her room and down the stairs, where she found her mother on the floor with her father wrapping his arms around her.

"What's wrong?" Claire demanded. Timothy, her father, shook his head and told her to wait. It took fifteen minutes before her mother quieted enough to be able to talk. Her mother had always been an overly dramatic person. Sometimes it pissed Claire off that her mother had no backbone. She had made a vow the day she'd come home from her kidnapping to never be like her mother. Mindy had been so hysterical, Timothy had to call the doctor to sedate her. She'd stayed doped up on pills for weeks afterward. No matter how many times Claire said she was fine, Mindy never believed her. Most of the time, Mindy lived in her head, where Claire suspected several demons resided.

Finally, after Mindy had calmed down, due to the pill the housekeeper handed Timothy, and her father had told Mindy to take. When she was settled back at the table, Timothy finally turned to his daughter. "Your mother answered the phone. You're grandfather passed away in his sleep last night."

Claire stood there in shock, and when Timothy went to hug her, she shrugged him off. "I'm okay. I knew it was coming." She wiped her tears, straightened her spine, and said, "At least I spent the day with him yesterday. He had a good day. We talked in his office. Do you need help with the funeral arrangements?"

Timothy stared at his daughter, and didn't know what to think about her practical attitude. Looking between his hysterical wife and calm as a cucumber daughter, he sighed and said, "Please. There's a folder in my bottom desk drawer with the information. We need to make the calls."

Claire went to her father's home office, and found the file. The first person she called was the nurse at her grandfather's home, and found out she'd already called for the coroner. Claire asked to speak with him if he was there.

"Hello?" a man said into the phone.

"Hello, my name is Claire Ambrose. I'm Albert's granddaughter. I just found out he passed. I understand you have your job to do. My only question is this... Do I call the funeral home, or do you?"

"I already called them. Because Mr. Ambrose died in his sleep, and he was at the end of his life, I'm only here to confirm he's gone. It's now up to the people in the funeral home to do their thing. Was there a need for an autopsy?"

"No, we know why he passed. It was cancer, and it was expected. Thank you for your time. Could you pass along for the funeral home to call me?"

"Yes, ma'am," the man said before he hung up. Claire looked up at her father as he entered his office.

"You, okay, Dad?"

"I guess. Your mother's a wreck. I feel numb. What did you find out?"

"The housekeeper called the police, who called the coroner, who called the funeral home. He's going to pass on the message for them to call us. I know Grandpa had everything done when Grandma died. It shouldn't be hard."

"I know," Timothy sighed as he settled in the chair across from his own desk. "What would I do without you, Claire?"

"Survive," she said firmly. "Dad, I won't be here forever. There will be a time when you and Mom need to grow a backbone and navigate this thing we call life. I may only be sixteen now, but I'm in college, and soon I'll be leaving to walk my own roads of life."

"I know, but don't let your mother hear you talk like that. Let's get over this one crisis first."

"Deal, but I'm warning you." She remained silent until her father looked at her.

"What's that?"

"All bets are off when I turn twenty-one."

"Deal. Stay here until then, and I'll back you one hundred percent on what you want to do."

"Thank you," she said as she stood, then went over to her father and hugged him tightly. "I'm sorry you lost your father."

"Thank you, but we knew it was coming."

"If it's any consolation, he had a great day yesterday. I found him in his office, we drank tea and talked. We even played a game of chess."

"Wow, that was a great day."

"It was. I'm glad that's my last memory of him." She kissed her father's cheek, then left the office to go to the kitchen to fix her breakfast.

CHAPTER FIVE
MAX

Max walked into his house and looked around. When he spotted his parents sitting in the living room reading, he paused for several minutes. After taking several deep breaths, he entered and sat down in the spot he always sat in, staring off into space. It was several minutes before anyone spoke.

"You okay, Son?" Kurt, Max's father, asked.

"I don't know," Max answered honestly, and stared at his father. "Can I talk to you?" He paused and looked at his mother, sitting on the other end of the couch. "Alone?"

"I'll go get dinner started," Elena said as she rose from her seat, and disappeared. Since the kitchen was on the other side of the house, there was no chance of his mother overhearing, but Max knew they would discuss it later. His parents discussed everything. Bracing himself, Max drew in a deep breath, let it out slowly, then moved over to the seat his mother had just vacated. This put him closer to his father, who sat in his lounge chair to his left.

"What's up?"

"I'm going to get right to the point. I've been having sex for the last three months."

"Oh, god," Kurt leaned forward in a panic. "Please tell me you used protection, and she's not pregnant?"

"What? No, she's not pregnant, and yes, I used a condom. I won't do it unless I have one. No matter how many times she says it's okay."

"Good," Kurt breathed out a sigh of relief and settled back in his chair. He could handle anything as long as his sixteen-year-old son hadn't gotten some girl pregnant. It was a long time before Max spoke again. Just when Kurt thought the conversation was over, Max spoke.

Max looked at his father directly in the eye and blurted, "Is it supposed to be blah?"

Kurt cocked his head to the side and frowned. "Blah? What do you mean, blah?"

"The sex. We do it, we get excited, and I know she has an orgasm, and I do, too. I even hold mine off until after she's done."

"Okay." Kurt nodded. "You're making sure your partner is taken care of. That's part of being a considerate lover."

"Thanks, I think. After I've done the deed, I don't feel like it was anything special. She's telling me how great it was, how terrific I am, but I don't feel anything."

"Nothing at all?"

"Well, the act feels good, as does the release, but I don't have the hearts and flowers feelings she says she has. I don't feel like I can shout my joy from the rooftops. It's just a 'meh' feeling. Something to relieve the pressure, nothing more." Max sat back and sighed heavily. "I don't know if it's me, her, or what." Max looked at his father, and Kurt saw the anguish in his eyes. "And I know I don't love this girl. I've told her. Bas and I are joining the Marines after we graduate, and I told her this. She said she's okay with it. But, if this is how sex makes you feel, then all those commercials, and romance books, are selling lies."

The father and son duo remained silent for several more minutes, before Max spoke again, "Don't get me wrong, I see how you and Mom are, and don't think I'm asking about your sex life, but I've heard you at times." At his father's shocked expression, Max grinned. "We have thin walls upstairs." Then, he laughed when Kurt's cheeks turned red. "And I've seen you the next morning. You have a bounce in your step, a huge grin on your face, and you and Mom are very affectionate with each other."

"That's called love, son."

"Is that why sex is so blah then? I don't love her?"

"It could be," Kurt admitted after several moments. "Son, sex can be the best thing in the world if you're with the right woman. If it's blah for you, then maybe your partner isn't the one for you. Your heart isn't involved. When it is, and you love each other, sex is an extension of your love, and it will make you feel like you can leap tall buildings, take on the world. It makes you feel powerful, but then, on the flip side, it can crush you and make you feel lost if the partner you love, either doesn't return that love, or if she does, but is hurt. That love will make you feel powerless to help her."

The two sat in silence, until Kurt cleared his throat, and asked, "Do you think you feel blah after sex, because you're not into women?"

Max whipped his head toward his father, wrinkled his nose, and said, "Eww, if you're asking if I'm gay, the answer is no. I've been in the locker room with several naked males, showering after a game or a practice. No way am I gay. Trust me on this."

"Okay," Kurt breathed a silent sigh of relief. Not that he wouldn't support his son in whatever gender he preferred, but he had to know if that might be the problem.

"Have you had sex with anyone besides the person you're having it with now?"

"No, just her." Max looked at his father and smirked. "And no, I'm not going to have sex with another woman to find out if it's the current one. I'm not like that."

Kurt laughed as he held up his hands. "I wasn't going to suggest that. I'm asking you to try to get to the root of your feelings." They both realized what he said and burst out laughing. That was how Elena found them when she stood in the doorway, and told them dinner was ready.

*****

LATER THAT NIGHT, WHILE Kurt and Elena lay in bed, Elena turned to her husband, and whispered, "Can you tell me what you and Max talked about earlier?"

Kurt rolled over onto his side, propped his head on his hand, and grinned at his wife. "Our son is having sex, and he asked me why it was blah."

Elena choked on her laughter. "Blah?"

"His word, not mine. Apparently, he does the deed, but doesn't feel anything but mild relief." Kurt told her of his entire conversation, and when he got to the part of the thin walls, Elena's cheeks turned bright red.

"He hears us?"

"So he says, but not all the time."

"Oh," Elena stared at her husband in shock, then began giggling when he grinned and raised his brows at her several times. A long time later, they lay wrapped in each other's arms, breathing deeply.

"So, what did you tell Max about feeling blah after sex?"

"First, I didn't say the exact words, but I asked if he was gay. He said no."

"He's not gay."

"I know, but I want to make sure he was okay with it in his head. Then, I asked if he loved this girl. He said no."

"Did you tell him he might feel better about sex if he loved her?"

"I did, but I don't think it did anything. He said sex still made him feel blah."

"Then he's not with the right partner." Elena snuggled with her husband, and as she dozed off, she frowned up at him. "I wonder."

"What?" Kurt murmured before he too fell asleep.

"I wonder if he can't feel anything, because he didn't do it with Bas. I'm not implying they're gay. Neither one of them are. It's just that they do everything together. Makes me wonder how he feels about sex. I work with a woman that has two husbands. They share her. Maybe that's something Max and Bas would benefit from. I'll talk to Marie about it later."

"No, let me talk to Oliver. We don't want to embarrass the boys more than we have to."

"Okay, love you," Elena whispered as she fell into a deep sleep.

*****

THE NEXT MORNING, KURT rose early and was sitting on his back porch when Oliver O'Grady walked up the back deck.

"Morning," they greeted each other, and Kurt leaned forward and filled a cup he'd brought out earlier.

"So, why did you want to see me at the ass crack of dawn?" Oliver groused as he settled in a chair and took a grateful sip of the hot brew. It wasn't even daylight yet. They had another hour before the sun even thought of rising.

"I don't mean to alarm you, but has Bas told you anything about him having sex?"

Oliver sputtered, spraying his sip of coffee all over the place. Glaring at his friend, he grabbed a napkin and wiped, not only his chin and shirt, but the surrounding table.

"No, are you telling me Max told you he's having sex?"

"I am. He came to me yesterday and asked me a question that floored me."

"And that was?"

"Why was sex so blah?" Kurt smirked into his hand with Oliver's reaction.

"He must not be doing it right then." Oliver grinned.

"I didn't exactly say that, but I told him because he didn't love the girl, then that might be the reason why."

"You think so?"

"Maybe, I'm not sure. My biggest fear when he told me he had been having sex for the last three months was that he had gotten a girl pregnant, but he reassured me that wasn't the case. As we talked, I flat-out asked if he was gay." Kurt held up his hand to ward off Oliver's statement. "I know he's not, and he confirmed it, but Elena said something that made me wonder. Hence the early morning meeting."

"I'm all ears."

"Do not take what I'm about to say as anything bad against your son, nor mine, but Elena wondered, because the boys are so close, if sex for Bas is blah, Max's exact words, was because Bas wasn't involved. She said something about a woman she works with has two husbands. That they share her, the coworker."

Kurt held his breath as he watched the expressions cross his friend's face. The final result wasn't what he'd expected. It was almost like acceptance.

"First, I do not think either one of our sons is gay, but I see what you mean about not being involved. Pat hasn't said anything to me about having sex. However, I know he is. I've smelled it on him when he's come home from a date. And it's hard to explain, but it seems like he's dejected when he comes home. Not all the time, but I bet you could pinpoint it to the fact that the boys both went on dates, but not together. If you follow me."

"I do. They had different agendas with their dates."

"Yeah." Both men were silent, and it was Oliver who leaned in, refilled both their cups, and studied Kurt.

"Do you think we should do what our fathers did for us?"

"Have you told anyone about that?"

"No, not even Marie."

"Same here, Elena doesn't know." They continued to sit there in silence, both lost in their own thoughts. "If we do this, how are we going to do it?" Kurt eventually asked.

"The same way our fathers did for us. We'll plan it, iron out the details, then take the boys fishing. We can go down to the cabin, drop them off, explain what's about to happen. After we find out if they're okay with it, then we head over to the nearest town and get a hotel room. Go back the next day."

"Works for me." Kurt nodded. "Only one thing. School's out in a month. Can we wait until then?"

"Absolutely." Oliver shook his head, and the two sat in silence, each lost in their own memories of a time long ago. Both had their own opinions of what would happen, and wouldn't voice them until then.

CHAPTER SIX
SEBASTIAN

"**D**ad, what type of fish are we going to be catching?" Bas asked from the back seat of his father's SUV. It was only five in the morning, and the four of them had been on the road for an hour, and still had two hours to go. The men had decided to make a long weekend of it. So, they had taken Thursday, Friday, and Monday off. It was just the four of them. After talking a month ago, both men had made plans for this weekend. School for the boys had let out only two days prior, and they wanted to get this trip over before they settled into their summer routine. Neither man knew how things would go, but they were willing to take either their sons' wrath or joy. Either way, they both believed this weekend had to occur.

"I don't think the salmon are running," Oliver said from the driver's seat. "But the others should be ready to catch."

"What others?" Max asked. "No offense to either of you, but this is the first time you've taken us fishing."

"No, it's not. Is it?" Kurt frowned as he turned in his seat to look at his son.

"I remember you took me fishing before I started kindergarten, but nothing after that," Max admitted.

"Oh." Kurt shook his head and looked at Oliver. The other man was no help when he smirked and shrugged.

"Well," Kurt said. "I'm sure there'll be catfish, crappie, bass, walleye, and others. We should reach the cabin in a couple of hours. We can put the boat in the water and start fishing then."

"Is there any place to stop for breakfast?" Bas asked as he rubbed his stomach, and before anyone could answer, both boys groaned when their stomachs growled. They didn't stop until they were almost at the cabin, not that they didn't want it, it was that nothing was open yet. They drove through a town and saw a small diner open. Oliver pulled in to park, and was surprised the boys waited for them. After using the facilities, they all grabbed a table in the middle of the dining room. It seemed like the outside booths were taken by the locals. Everyone nodded to them, or lifted their coffee cup in greeting.

The waitress, a woman in her thirties, approached with menus. "Morning, what can I do get you to drink?" All four of them ordered coffee, but then the boys ordered large glasses of orange juice. The waitress hurried away, then was back with a tray with their drinks. After placing their order, she didn't bat an eye when it came to what the boys ordered. Each asked for a large western omelet with home fries, a side of bacon, as well as an order of sausage gravy over biscuits. Their fathers only shook their heads, smirked, and looked at each other.

"Remember when we used to eat like that?"

"Yeah, those were the days when we didn't have to worry about high blood pressure, cholesterol, or the threat of diabetes." Kurt shook his head as he sighed, and studied his son, who only grinned.

"Hey, boys, it seems like it's been a long time since it's only been the four of us. You're getting older, and that's why we decided on this weekend." Oliver began. "I feel like we haven't really sat down and talked since Max's unfortunate accident three years ago."

Bas snorted a laugh. "Unfortunate accident? Don't you mean when we were young, dumb, and thought we were invincible?"

"That too," the men laughed. "I have to say, I'm proud that neither one of you went back to your daredevil ways."

"Spending three months in a wheelchair was enough for us," Bas said. "Though I didn't sit on my ass all summer, the punishment was enough to make me realize that taking risks is okay, but only if the rewards are greater than the risks. I want to be around after I graduate from high school to do what I want out of life."

"Me too. That one mistake made me realize that life is for living, not stupid stunts," Max said as he rubbed his collar bone. "I never thought I'd heal."

"Isn't it time for you boys to start thinking about colleges? You just finished your sophomore year. Congratulations, by the way. I'm proud of both of you for making the high honor roll."

"Thanks," the boys answered at the same time. They looked at each other, then at their fathers. They did this a couple of times, and it was Bas who spoke first.

"Actually, we're not going to college, not right away."

"Why not?" Oliver demanded, but they had to put the conversation on hold until the waitress finished delivering their food.

Once they had their coffee refilled and seasoned everything, they began to dig in. To Oliver and Kurt, it seemed like the boys inhaled half the omelet in one bite. The talk was put on hold until they finished one dish, then turned to the second. Downing half his juice, Bas wiped his mouth, then looked at his father.

"Sorry, but I was hungry."

"Don't worry about it, but why aren't you going to college? You're both smart, you get excellent grades. You play sports, you've run your own leaf and snow removal business for the last three years, so any school would be glad to have you."

"We know." The boys grinned at their fathers. "But, we're going to join the Marines. If we want to go to college, we'll do it on Uncle Sam's dime, with the GI bill."

The men sat there in stunned silence. "The Marines?"

"Yep."

"Wow," Kurt shook his head as he studied both boys. "That's hard-core."

"We know." They grinned as they devoured the rest of their food. The shocking part of the whole interaction was when the bill arrived and Bas picked up the check before Oliver or Kurt could. "We got this." They grinned at their fathers' expressions.

When the two boys went up to the register to pay, Oliver looked at Kurt, and said, "I think we're raising two very well-adjusted boys."

"Yeah, me too. I just thank the Lord they woke up and didn't go back to their daredevil ways after Max healed."

"You and me both, friend," Oliver said as he slapped Kurt on the shoulder. "You and me both." They left the restaurant and climbed back into the SUV. Just before they reached the cabin, Bas spoke from the back seat.

"Hey, Dad. If we don't catch any fish, at least that diner is close enough, we won't starve." That set everyone off laughing, which set the tone for the next two days.

*****

"READY?" KURT ASKED Oliver mid-morning on Saturday.

"Not really, but we should get this over with. At least we had two wonderful days with the boys. I don't know about you, but I've enjoyed myself. It was a real treat to be able to teach my son how to flay a fish."

"Yeah, never thought we'd catch as much as we did. It's a skill they'll have for the rest of their lives, and I'm happy to be able to give it to them."

Oliver nodded as they walked up the shoreline to their cabin. It was a cabin that had belonged to the O'Grady family for generations. It was so remote that no one really came here anymore. Oliver's grandfather had been born there. It wasn't much bigger than a two-room shack, but it had all the amenities, like running water and electricity. The family had hired a local couple to come out once a week to check on things. Eventually, it'd be passed down in the family. Because the eldest Sebastian O'Grady still lived, and didn't show any signs of kicking it anytime soon, it was still in his possession, then it'd get passed to Oliver's father, then to Oliver, then to Pat, and down the line.

The men entered the kitchen through the deck door, and smiled as both boys, barefoot, shirtless, and dressed in sweats, with their hair sticking up all over the place, stumbled into the room. The first thing they did was open the refrigerator, and while one grabbed the bottle of orange juice, the other the apple juice, not bothering with a glass, they opened the containers and chugged.

"Glasses!" Kurt yelled, and only got a grunt in response. They didn't stop drinking until they'd finished the half-full bottles. Once they put them down, they looked at each other, grinned, then looked at their fathers.

"Why?" they asked as they chucked the empty containers into the recycling bin by the back door. "Can we go down to the diner for breakfast?" Bas asked as he rubbed his growling stomach. The older adults exchanged looks, then nodded.

"Getting tired of fish?" Oliver laughed as he asked.

"Yeah, don't get me wrong, I love eating what we catch, and it's probably healthy for us, but three solid days, no thanks."

"Go get changed," Kurt said as he watched the boys high five themselves, and take off at a run. He looked at Oliver with a raised brow.

"We have time."

"I know, way to stick to our guns about not deviating from our plans." He smirked at Oliver's chuckle. In under ten minutes the four of them were climbing into the SUV, and heading into town. Two hours later, they were back and they all lounged around the unlit firepit, too full from breakfast to move.

Oliver cleared his throat several times, and finally sat forward with his forearms on his knees. "Boys."

"Yeah," they mumbled with their eyes half-closed, staring into what should be a fire. Kurt jumped to his feet, grabbed a stick they had been using on the fire at night, and saw hot embers beneath the ash. He stirred it up and threw on some kindling. In no time, a nice fire blazed.

"Boys," Oliver said more firmly, and when they looked at him, he let his breath out slowly. "Kurt and I need to discuss something with you."

"What's that?" Bas asked.

Not wanting to wait any longer, Oliver looked directly into his son's eyes and asked, "Are you having sex with your girlfriends?"

Oliver expected his son to deny it or get all huffy, but instead he released a heavy sigh, slumped in his chair and said, "Yeah."

"And?"

"And what? I'm having sex, I use protection. What's the big deal?"

"How does it make you feel?"

"Huh?" Bas stared at his father in confusion. "What do you mean? How does it make me feel?"

"Max," Kurt spoke for the first time. "Why don't you tell Bas what you told me?"

Max glared at his father, then turned to look at his best friend. "I'm having sex too, and though she says she enjoys it, and I ejaculate, it's like blah. Nothing you read about or hear about. Nothing spectacular. At this point, I could give it up and it wouldn't bother me."

Everyone stared at Bas as he deflated before their very eyes. "Thank god! I thought it was me."

"What do you mean?" Oliver asked. "And this conversation stays here. This is the main reason why we brought you boys here." That statement seemed to relax the boys and they discussed in great detail how they'd help their girlfriends enjoy sex, but they didn't enjoy it.

At one point Bas sighed, rubbed his face, and admitted, "Sometimes, I feel like I'm only performing a duty. You know. I don't get the high, or whatever the hell it's called when I have sex." He sighed heavily and slumped back in his chair, staring at the fire.

It was a long time, almost twenty minutes, before Oliver spoke again, "Boys." He waited until he had their full attention. Only then did he start his tale. "As you know, Kurt and I grew up like you two are now. Close, best friends, inseparable."

"Yeah," Bas agreed as he frowned at his father. He leaned forward and threw another log on the fire. Though it was almost noon, it was a gray and overcast day. Because of what Oliver and Kurt needed to say to the boys, they had opted not to go fishing that day. They would resume that tomorrow.

"What about it?" Max prompted, when Oliver stopped talking.

"Oliver's father brought us both to this cabin when we were your age," Kurt took up the story.

"Yeah, so?" Bas shrugged it off. "What are you trying to say? That we started a tradition?"

"Not really," Kurt said, then jumped to his feet and poked the fire again. Max sat up and started paying attention.

"Dad, are you nervous about something?" Max asked, as he looked at Bas, then over at Oliver. The boys watched as Kurt drew a deep breath of air into his lungs, then let it out slowly.

"Yeah, so I'm just going to say this. We brought you here for some father/son bonding, but there's another reason why we brought you here."

"Which is?" Bas encouraged, and waved his hand in a hurry-up motion.

"Tonight, Oliver and I will go into town to dinner. Afterward, we're going to a hotel. We've already booked two rooms for tonight, which we booked before coming here, and we'll be staying there tonight."

Oliver had been watching the boys closely, and when it looked like they were about to say something, he spoke firmly, "Alone. You two will spend the night here, like the last couple of nights."

"Why?" Bas frowned at the adults.

Oliver scrubbed his face, and blurted out, "There's a woman coming tonight who is going to teach you hands-on experience." At their frowns, he felt his cheeks heat as he said, "Sexual experiences. Just the two of you and her."

"Together?" Both boys looked at their fathers in shock. "But, we're not gay."

"We know that. But some men enjoy sharing a woman. Both your father and I have a couple of friends that do this. They even married her, though she couldn't be married to each man simultaneously, there is a whole community that they are involved in. There are ways in the eyes of the people that acknowledge that she is married to each of them, though according to the law, she's only married to one of them. But, they are married, and the three of them have a sexual relationship. They even have children together."

"That sounded bad," Kurt laughed. He turned to his son, and said, "Though I hate to admit this, but remember the conversation we had about you thinking sex was blah? I told your mother about that talk. She suggested that maybe because you boys are so close, so tight, you might enjoy sharing a woman. That's why we're here this weekend. The last two days were so we could get to know you better. It feels like we don't see you anymore, but tonight is for you. We'll give you the cabin and the woman will arrive at seven. You don't have to do anything. We told her that already."

"She's basically going to ask you questions and then answer any that you might have. Like hands-on sex education," Oliver stated as he stared at the boys, then looked at Kurt for his reaction.

Several minutes later, Bas was the first one to voice any concern.

"Is she a prostitute?"

"*No*," Kurt said as he went back and sat beside Oliver. "She's a woman that is in the lifestyle."

"What's that mean? In the lifestyle?"

"Jasmine's been in a ménage relationship a couple of times. She can tell you all about it. What works, and what didn't work for her."

"Has she been tested for any diseases?" Max asked, then shrugged. "Hey, you never know."

"Good questions, boys," Oliver nodded. "It proves that you're thinking clearly on this matter. However, these will have to be questions for you to ask her. We don't know and don't want to give you false information."

The boys nodded, then looked at each other, shrugged, and grinned. "What's it going to hurt?" Bas asked.

"Nothing, I guess," Max answered with his own smirk. Then he looked directly at his best friend and said, "Remember to keep your junk away from me."

"Same to you, buddy, same to you."

Oliver and Kurt exchanged grins and relaxed, knowing they'd done the right thing. They spent the rest of the afternoon around the cabin and by five that night, the adults left to go to town, saying they would be back around eight the next morning.

CHAPTER SEVEN
MAX

Max sat on the spare bed in the bedroom and studied his best friend intently. After several minutes of silence, he asked, "So, what do you think?"

Bas looked at Max in the mirror and then turned to look at him. "I don't know yet. You?"

"Honestly? Scared, intrigued, nervous. The one thing that I know I'm not feeling is weirded out. You know?"

"Yeah, I do. I think if I'm going to do this, I'd want it to be with you."

"I know, and it doesn't seem strange." Max nodded to his friend, looked at his feet, then said, "Turn around and look at me." When Bas did, Max stood, and said, "We tell *no one* about this. Only the five of us will know this was discussed. But, only us two, and this woman will know what did, or did not happen. I don't know about you, but I don't need rumors to start that we're gay."

"I agree." Bas held out his hand, and they did their own secret handshake to seal the promise. "This is our private life. No one needs to know except the woman we're with and us.

"Agreed." Max nodded. "I also want to put something out there."

"What?"

"If something happens and we end up having sex with this woman, then I want us to be perfectly honest with each other. If one of us gets uncomfortable at any time, then we say so. Don't just continue if we think the other is having a good time. Speak up. Be honest from the beginning."

"I agree." Again they did their special handshake and looked at themselves one last time in the mirror, and went out into the main room of the cabin. Bas rubbed his stomach, and asked, "I wonder what Dad and Kurt are eating right now?"

Max threw his head back and laughed. "You're always thinking of your stomach first."

"Hey, I'm a growing boy."

Laughing, they raided the refrigerator of the leftover pizza from earlier that day. By the time they had finished and cleaned up after themselves, there was a knock on the door.

Spilling his drink in surprise, Max looked at Bas with wide eyes. Bas looked back at him with panic in his. They both closed their eyes, drew in a deep breath, and let it out slowly.

"We got this," they said at the same time, and fist-bumped each other. Max went and opened the door, while Bas stayed near the kitchen table.

"Hello," Max said as he opened the door to a beautiful woman. He hadn't expected someone so young. He thought it would be someone his father's age. "Are you Jasmine?"

"I am."

"Come in," Max said as he stepped back, and watched Bas's face as the woman entered. Max grinned when he saw interest and approval coming from his best friend. After shutting the door, Max turned to her, and just stood there like an idiot.

Jasmine gave a soft laugh, and said, "Why don't we get to know each other first? We have no time limit and I don't expect anything from either of you." Her statement deflated them and they both looked at each other, and after inviting her to sit, Bas got them all drinks. It turned out to be apple juice, because they were too young to drink alcohol, and Jasmine declined a beer.

Max sat on the couch with Bas on the other end. The three of them silently looked at each other.

"Okay," Jasmine chuckled, "I guess I'll start. What did your fathers tell you about me?"

"That you were in the lifestyle," Bas blurted out.

"What's that mean?" Max asked.

"Okay, let me tell you about myself. But first, you have to promise that this stays here. Nothing we say or may do leaves this cabin. I could get in a lot of trouble for this."

"How?"

"You two are only sixteen, right?" At their nods, she said, "I'm twenty-three. I could be arrested and thrown in jail if anyone found out. I'm not saying we're going to have sex. That's all up to you. But, I'm saying you have to keep your mouths shut."

"Oh, we already made a pact that whatever happens here, stays here," Max said.

"Okay, then." Jasmine drew in a breath and let it out slowly. "The only information I received before I was asked to come here was that there were two young boys that thought sex was blah." She smirked when the boys' faces turned beet red. Chuckling, she leaned over and patted each of their hands, then settled back in her chair. She had worn a nice blouse with her favorite pair of jeans, not really expecting anything to happen, so she had wanted to be comfortable, not sexy.

"As I said, my name is Jasmine. Let's not say our last names. Who are you?"

"Max."

"Bas."

"Bas? What type of name is that?"

"Short for Sebastian."

"Oh, okay. And is Max short for anything?"

"Max."

"Fair enough. Okay, as I said, I'm Jasmine, and I'm bi-sexual. That means I like both men and women." When they didn't seem shocked or asked any questions, she continued. "I've been in two serious ménage relationships in my life. The first one was when I was nineteen, and it was two men and me. It lasted for a year, but they were older than me by at least ten years. When they started talking about having babies and settling down, I couldn't do it. I was still going to college, and didn't know what I wanted to do with my life. While it hurt us to part, it didn't break us. I hope you can understand the difference."

"I do," Bas said, and looked at Max.

"Me too. It was sad, but it didn't rip your heart out. You were able to still see them without wanting to kill them."

"Exactly. I saw them just last week, and I'm happy to say they've found what they were looking for. I met her and she's wonderful for them. Oh, in case you're wondering, they were both males. Best friends." She covered her smirk when the two boys before her looked at each other.

"And the other relationship?" Max asked.

"Now that one broke me." She exhaled and sipped her juice, then with a shaking hand, set it back down. "This time, I was already in a relationship with another woman. For privacy reasons, I won't mention any names, but we were in a committed relationship. She was bi also. But, something was missing. One night, we met a man at the club and asked him to join us to do a scene there at the club." Looking at them, she saw confusion on their faces. "The club I'm referring to is a BDSM club I'm a member of. It's private and hard to get into. There's a long waitlist. Once you're in, there are all sorts of NDAs to sign and rules to follow. Not just the sex rules either, protocol of how to act in the club, and towards its members, but in the long run, it's for everyone's safety."

Max and Bas nodded and settled into their seats to listen to her.

"Anyway, my partner and I loved each other and had been exclusive since we began the relationship. One night we agreed to spice things up and invited this gentleman to join us. That one scene turned into something more." She paused and rubbed her forehead. With a faraway look in her eyes, she continued quietly. At first, Max and Bas had to lean forward to hear her.

"All three of us enjoyed ourselves that night. After a few days, she and I began talking and decided to ask him to be our third. We didn't see him at the club until two months later. Since he was a member, we knew he was safe. We asked to scene with him again. He agreed. After the scene," she stopped when Max held up his hand.

"What's a scene?"

"The foreplay and build-up to sex."

"You have sex in this club?" Bas asked in shock.

Jasmine smirked. "Well, it is a sex club, so yeah."

"Oh," both their faces turned red again.

"Sorry, but I couldn't resist." Jasmine laughed, then settled back in her seat. "Over the next month, the three of us met outside the club, had drinks, or dinner. We talked about having a more personal relationship with the three of us, but it would be exclusive."

"Meaning?"

"Meaning the sex would involve only us three—him and me, him and her, us and him. No one else could join in. Not in our homes, nor at the club. We became inseparable for the next year." She looked off into space, and Max was the one to reach out and touch her hand.

"What happened?"

"Things started changing. They were subtle at first. I didn't really catch on."

"Can you tell us what they were?" Bas asked.

"I'd come home and find the two of them in bed together, which wasn't anything unusual. We'd have sex together or separately all the time, but when they started sleeping together in the same bed, was when I realized something was wrong. If I'd come home from work and they'd be together, they wouldn't want sex that night. When we were together, it was like they weren't connected to me like they had been. I felt like they were pushing me away. When I'd say something to her, she'd deny it. That was the hardest part."

"What happened?"

"I came home one night after a very rough week at work, and found them dressed to the nines, getting ready to go out.

When I asked where we were going, because our whole relationship before me being pushed aside was the three of us did everything together. They flat-out told me I wasn't invited. Shocked the shit out of me. As I stood there stunned, they turned to leave. In my anger I said that if they didn't tell me what was going on, then I'd be gone by the time they returned."

"Oh no," Max said with his eyebrows buried in his hairline.

"Yeah, she turned and looked at me over her shoulder and said, 'That would be great, thanks.'"

"Oh, shit, what did you do?"

"Well, I started to pack my things, then I realized that the apartment was in my name. Remember that first relationship I told you about? The ones with the two guys? They bought it for me as a parting gift. I only had to pay the utilities. She moved in with me. He moved in with us."

"Please, tell us you packed their shit and not yours."

"I did," Jasmine laughed. She stood and paced. "It was epic, they walked back in, and I was sitting on the living-room couch. I used every suitcase and duffel bag I could find and stuffed their things in them. Hell," she gave a mirthless laugh. "I even used garbage bags and cardboard boxes. Anyway, they came home all giddy and had their hands all over each other. They were halfway through the living room when I turned on the light. It had been dark when they entered."

"Why do I see a train wreck coming?" Max asked with a grin.

"No, not quite a train wreck. The whole time I packed everything, I was seething, but by the time they returned, I'd calmed down enough to be rational. I had even made a copy of the agreement I had with the gentlemen who bought the apartment, ready to show them. I say copy, because there was no way in hell I'd give them the original document for them to tear to shreds. She was like that when she became angry. I needed to prove the place was mine. Not only that..." Jasmine grinned at them, "I called the gentlemen and explained what had happened. They said to pack my roommate's stuff, and if they didn't leave to call them, and they'd come set them straight."

She paced a few more times, then sat back down. "What I didn't tell you was that they, my former boyfriends, had met her. After that first time, they'd contacted me and asked what I was doing with her. They didn't like her at all. That was based on only meeting her once."

"First impressions," Bas said as he nodded.

"Yes, but I told them I loved her. Anyway, after I turned on the light, she turned on me and started screaming that I should have left by then. Very loudly, and rudely, she explained that I was the third wheel in the relationship. They realized they loved each other, and they wanted me out of the relationship, but I was too stupid to understand that. Then she tried to bully me off the couch."

"What did you do?"

"I looked at him and asked him to tell me in his own words what he thought. He echoed everything she said. I'll be honest, I shed tears. And as my heart was breaking, I pointed to the other side of the living room and told them as coldly as I could. 'There are your things. Give me your key before you leave. But I'm having the locks changed anyway.'"

"Shit, what happened next?"

"She walked over and called the police. They came, and after both of them told them of the situation, the police turned to me, and I only handed them a piece of paper. It was priceless. The cops read it, turned to the two of them and said, 'It's her apartment. She has every right to kick you out.'"

"What happened next?"

"Both of them ended up being arrested, because she flew through the room and attacked me. When I got away, he slapped me across the face for being a bitch. His words, not mine. Right in front of the cops. That was a little over a year ago. I think I'm more bitter than angry."

"Have you been in a relationship since?"

"No, I don't know what I'm looking for. But the next relationship I enter into, I want the rules laid down. Like I did with my first one."

"What's that mean?"

"I might be assuming here, but say the two of you want to share your women. There's nothing wrong with that, not at all, and it doesn't make you a freak. Before I leave, I'll give you each a card with the name of someone to call if you have any questions. If I've learned anything, it's that communication is the key. Without that, you'll end up like I did—almost tossed out of my own home. Talk with each other, know your expectations, what you want out of a relationship, what you don't."

"What's that mean?"

"Are you gay?"

"No!" They both said as one.

"Okay, then you don't want the other's junk anywhere near you. That's how it was with my first relationship. I asked them why they do ménage, and they both admitted that sex separately didn't fulfill them like having a woman between them did. Something about not feeling complete unless they could pleasure her at the same time. At first, I thought it was an ego thing, but since having been between the two of them and separately, I can attest to that. There was something about them that they could read what the other wanted. If one stumbled in pleasuring me, the other brought him back." She chuckled. "I'll be honest, I didn't see what they did, but I sure felt it." With a smile on her face, she gave a little shudder and looked at them.

"Do you have any questions?"

The three of them stayed up all night talking. Though they didn't do anything, both Max and Bas had all their questions answered. The three of them were making breakfast when Oliver and Kurt returned. The older men were taken aback seeing the woman sitting at the table, while their sons waited on her.

"Everything okay?" Kurt asked.

"Yep," they all said, and resumed what they had been doing. Max looked up, and asked, "Did you guys eat?"

"Yeah, we stopped at the diner on the way here," Oliver said, but he accepted the cup of coffee from his son. An hour later, the boys walked Jasmine to her car, and they both gave her a kiss on the cheek.

She opened her purse and handed them each two business cards. "One is mine. If you ever want to hook up, let me know. If I'm in a relationship, I'm sure I can find something for you, but please, be at least eighteen."

The boys laughed and promised they would be. "And the second card?" Max asked as he looked at the black card with only a phone number printed in gold.

"That's to a gentleman that will answer any more questions you may have. He's the owner of the club I told you about. He's big on educating people about the lifestyle. His motto is the more informed, the less likely to hurt someone, or something like that." She sighed as she studied the two young men.

"I like you, boys. I wish you well in whatever you do in your lives. If by any chance you do join the Marines, I'm going to thank you now for serving our country. And you come home safe." She stood on tiptoe and kissed each of their cheeks, then climbed in her car and drove away.

"You know?" Max looked at Bas with a grin. "I feel comfortable with not doing it with Jasmine. Somehow it didn't seem right."

"I know, but I'm glad we asked all those questions." Bas nodded to his friend. "I do know a few things."

"What's that?"

"One, there's no way Sally or Janette would want a ménage. Two, I wouldn't want to do it with anyone we have to see every day. It would be too weird."

"Yeah, and that would ruin our promise to keep this to ourselves. No, if we ever decide to do this, we need to do it away from home."

"Agreed," Bas held out his hand, and they locked hands on the other's forearm. They looked at each other and grinned.

"Should we fuck with our dads?"

"How?" Bas frowned.

"By not saying anything about last night." Max grinned, and the two of them burst out laughing. They walked back and saw the men in question, and Max called out. "Ready to go fishing?" Max and Bas looked at their fathers and grinned. They could both see that each man had questions, but they weren't about to reveal what had happened the night before. Even if it was only talking, this was theirs to keep, not to share.

CHAPTER EIGHT
CLAIRE

Claire Ambrose walked into the kitchen of her parents' house and walked directly to the coffee pot. After pouring herself a cup, she joined her parents at the table. It was mid-morning on a Saturday. For the last two weeks, she'd been working overtime at her job, as well as having several conversations with people far away from here.

After several conversations and more phone calls, she'd finally come to a decision. She wanted to avoid World War III as much as possible, but knew without a doubt, because of her mother, it wouldn't be possible. She just needed to state her case, and not give in to her mother's tears. Firming her spine, she settled in her customary chair, and because her stomach was already in knots, she avoided the food laid out on the table.

"I have an announcement to make," Claire said, after almost five minutes of silence.

"What's that, dear?" her mother asked, but Claire knew she wasn't really listening.

"I'm moving out."

"No!" Her mother looked up from the fashion magazine she'd been thumbing through, to yell, "Over my dead body."

"Well, at least I can do the autopsy on you," Claire snarled at her. "There's nothing you can do about it, Mother. I'm twenty-one, legally an adult." She knew not to dump all her information at once when it came to her mother.

"I forbid it," Mindy Ambrose said as she slammed her open palm on the table, causing the dishes to jump.

"Now, Mindy, let's hear her out." Timothy reached over and patted his wife's hand. It took everything Claire had not to roll her eyes.

"Why do you forbid it, Mom? Tell me one good reason why you won't let me live my life my way. If you can convince me to stay, then I will. Until then, know that after this conversation, I'm going to my room to finish packing my things." Claire propped her chin on her hand and stared at her mother.

"You could be kidnapped. It happened before."

"When Grandpa was alive, and a judge on the bench, and that was fifteen years ago."

"What about those two boys that were kidnapped? They never found them."

"They were boys, it happened six years ago, and it was on the other side of the state, nowhere near here." She kept her gaze steady on her mother. "Next."

"What about your job?"

"What about it? The way people keep killing each other, I'll always have a job." Claire winced when she said that. She had never told her parents exactly what she did for a living. Before they could comment, she held up her hand. "I've contacted several people and have a new job starting two weeks from Monday. I've already put in my two weeks' notice, and it was accepted. I'm leaving Monday for the new job. My new boss gave me several recommendations for apartments in the area."

"I want to know where you're going. What's your job? Who's your boss? What will you be doing? Who do you report to? Who will you be working with? What town?"

"When I get settled, I'll give you all that information. Until then, you'll have to do something for once in your life."

"What's that?"

"Trust me." Claire had looked directly at her mother when she said it. When the woman didn't react, Claire knew she was doing the right thing by moving to a different state. Her father catered to her mother, and her mother was the biggest worrywart that lived. Everything that happened in the world would affect Claire, so she tried to keep her home and not allow her out of the house, but Claire had put her foot down when she went to college at a young age. She had been tested young and found she was smart. She currently held two PhDs and a Master's.

"I can't do that." Mindy glared at her daughter.

"Then, *I* can't tell you where I'm going. Not only am I an adult at the state level, but also at the federal level. Go ahead, call the cops. They'll only laugh in your face. And..." Claire paused until her mother looked directly at her "...in case you forgot, I work for the police department. They'd never arrest me, or whatever you think I need." Claire rose to her feet, carried her untouched coffee to the sink, and dumped it. She then rinsed her cup and placed it in the dishwasher. "I have work to do."

"I FORBID YOU FROM LEAVING THIS HOUSE!" Mindy jumped to her feet and screamed. "Timothy, tell her. It's not safe out there. She needs to stay where she's safe."

"Mindy, it's time to let her go. Claire is an adult. She's well-educated, smart, and has a good sense about her. I trust her."

"You're taking her side in this?" Mindy glared at her husband, then stormed off. "I refuse to be ganged up on in my own home." As she left the room, she quickly turned on her heel and glared at her daughter.

"If you defy me, your mother, then once you walk out this door, you're not welcome back." Then she turned back around and stormed off. Both Claire and her father waited until they heard a door slam, then she turned to him to smirk. "Sorry."

"Don't worry about it. I knew this was coming for years. Do you really have a job to go to?"

"Yes, I'm going to be the supervisor of the crime lab. It's a small police agency, but they have a crime lab. No offense, but I'll call you when I'm settled."

"I understand. Do you need any help? Do you need any money?"

"I'm good. I've been saving my paycheck since I started working two years ago, and in a pinch, I have the money Grandpa left me. I still haven't touched that."

"Let me know if you need anything." Timothy walked to his daughter and hugged her. "I'm just sorry your mother can't see how wonderful you are."

"Her loss." Claire shrugged, then hugged her father back. "I'll be in my room." She left and went to her room. It didn't take long to pack her things. The hardest part was carrying everything down to load up her SUV. She would have asked her father to help, but her mother had come out of her room, and demanded that he take her away from her disappointing daughter.

After everything was packed, she took a shower and packed her dirty clothes in a bag to take with her. Satisfied she had everything, Claire finally walked into her father's office and left the note she'd written to him. It contained all the information her mother demanded of her. If she knew her mother, she had ordered her father to take her to the police station and find out where Claire was moving to.

After placing the note in her and her father's spot, she took one last stroll around the house and found her charger, as well as her e-reader. Satisfied, she took her house key off her ring, laid it on the counter, then picked up her purse, and walked out of her childhood home.

"I will be back," she whispered before she closed the door, climbed in her vehicle, and headed to her new destination.

CHAPTER NINE
MAX

"Ready?" Sebastian asked Max as they walked toward two separate rooms, each holding a folder. They were about to get their physicals, because they were in the process of joining the Marines. They had to do the physical test, then the mental, and they were good to go. If everything went as planned, in less than two weeks, they'd be heading to Parris Island, South Carolina.

An hour later, Max looked up when a knock sounded on the door, and a doctor walked in.

"Mr. Abbott, I'm Dr. Harris."

"Hey, Dr. Harris, how's it going?"

"Good."

"How'd I do?"

"Good, your blood pressure is perfect, as well as your cholesterol and your blood work. You are a perfectly healthy eighteen-year-old. Plus being six foot four, and two hundred pounds, excellent health."

Max frowned at the man and drew in a deep breath to let out slowly. "But? I feel there's a but in there somewhere."

"But, you are not eligible to join the Marines, or any branch of the military."

"What? You just said I was healthy. Why not?"

"You have foreign objects in your body." Dr. Harris turned and slapped several x-rays up on the light and turned it on. He pointed to the left ankle. "Here."

"Yeah, I got those when I was thirteen."

"May I ask how?"

Max felt his cheeks heat. "My best friend and I made a ramp. I was the first one down it. We live about five miles outside Bonner's Ferry. It's already mountain territory, but the ramp added extra height." He laughed when the doctor chuckled. "When I landed, it was on my left ankle, it shattered, then I went ass over tea kettle and broke my collarbone." He reached up and touched it, and the doctor took down one of the foot x-rays and put up another one.

"I see," Harris said. He studied them, then pulled a piece of paper and passed it to Max. "Read the highlighted area."

Max took the paper, frowned, then read. After reading it several times, Max looked up and demanded. "Are you serious?"

"As a heart attack, and if you look," Dr. Harris tapped the top of the page. "It pertains to all branches of the military."

"Son of a bitch," Max said, dejected. He studied the x-rays in front of him, and it took everything he had not to cry.

"So this is it?"

"As far as the military is concerned, yes. Was there something else you wanted to do?"

"Not really." Max scrubbed his face then exhaled heavily. "Do you think I can become a cop?"

"I don't see why not. Their restrictions aren't as strict as the military. If you'd like, I can give you a copy of today's physical. Might save you the hassle."

Dr. Harris put his hand on Max's shoulder and gave a gentle squeeze. "I'm really sorry about your military career."

"Thanks, nothing to do now." Max waited until the doctor left, then he hopped off the exam table and dressed. At this point, he didn't know if he was pissed or sad, but one thing, he was definitely disappointed.

Since he couldn't join the Marines, and Bas would be tied up all day, Max walked to the library three blocks down and started his research. It turned out that he couldn't join the police academy until he was twenty-one. That gave him three years to find something to do. Not wanting the grass to grow under his feet, he went back to the testing center and grabbed Bas's truck. On a hunch he drove out to the high school he'd graduated from three weeks ago.

"Max, how are you?" Mrs. Fox, the school secretary, looked at him in surprise.

"Hey, Mrs. Fox. I know this is an odd request, but is Mr. Hunt in?"

"Sure, let me call him." She picked up the phone, and after she hung up, she smiled at the young man. "Go on down to his office."

"Thanks, Mrs. Fox." Max turned on his heel and strode out. Seeing Mr. Hunt down the hall, he hurried his steps. As he came abreast of his former guidance counselor, Max stuck out his hand. After the greetings, they went into the office and settled in their seats.

"This is a surprise, Max. What brings you here?"

"I need some advice."

"Okay. With?"

"I just came from my physical for the Marines."

"Really, why are you here? I know you and Sebastian talked about joining the Marines. What happened?"

"Bas is still there, at the testing center. I had my physical and had to have whole body x-rays. Turned out I'm not eligible for any branch of the military, especially not the Marines."

"Why not?" Mr. Hunt leaned forward in his shock. Placing his hands on his desk, he studied the younger man.

"I had an accident when I was thirteen. Shattered my ankle. I have pins and plates in it. Because the military classifies that as foreign objects, I'm not eligible."

"Wow, I never knew that. What are you going to do now?"

"That's why I'm here. Because of the Marines, I never filled out any college applications. If I can't join, then I'd like to become a cop. Unfortunately, I have to be twenty-one before I can even apply. That's three years away. I wondered if maybe you could recommend colleges I can get in and start with a criminology degree. If I went for a Master's I'd be twenty-two when I started the academy. It would give me something to do until then." Max held up his hand and sighed. "I'm not going to flip burgers until then. I'd even be willing to start in January if September is too soon."

"Can you give me a couple of days to call some of my contacts? Let me make sure I have your contact information." Max gave it to him, made his way out of the school and back to the testing center. He waited in the truck for another two hours until Bas joined him. Max let his best friend talk about everything he had gone through. As much as he wanted to ask questions, he found he couldn't. All he wanted to do right now was scream at himself for his stupidity from years ago.

Thankfully, Bas had something to do that afternoon, and Max dropped him off, jumped into his own truck, and headed to his home. He sat in the driver's seat for a long time. It wasn't until his father knocked on his window that he came back into himself.

Getting out of the truck, he remained silent until his mother told him to wash up for supper. After they settled at the table, Max found he wasn't hungry and moved his plate aside. He leaned back and looked at his parents. "I might as well tell you. Your son is a first-class fucking idiot. Sorry for swearing, but it's true."

"What happened?" Elena asked as she put her hand over her son's, shocked when he gripped hers hard.

"Did you know that because of my stupidity, I'm only not allowed to join the Marines, but I can't join any branch of the military?"

"Why the hell not?" Kurt demanded.

"Like I said, my stupidity."

"Son," Kurt said as he reached over and put his hand over his and Elena's. "There was only one time in your whole life you were stupid. When you decided to ride a ramp down the mountain."

"Ding, ding, ding, you got it in one. Give the man a cigar," Max said so sarcastically, both his parents reared back, but didn't lose their grip on his hand.

"What happened?" Elena asked gently.

"The military classifies those pins and plates as foreign objects. Because of those, I'm not eligible to join."

"Shit," Kurt said. "So what are you going to do now?"

"While Bas was getting his testing done, I went to the library and did some research, then I went back to the center, borrowed Bas's truck, and went to the high school."

"Why?" both his parents asked.

"I researched getting into the police academy. One downfall, I have to be twenty-one."

"That's three years away."

"Yes, so I went and talked to Mr. Hunt. Told him everything I found out. I gave him my contact information, and he's going to make some calls. I'm going to try to enroll in college for Criminology. I figure if I get my Master's that's four years, then I'll be twenty-two. Plenty of time to join the academy, and I'll have the education to boot."

"Wow." Elena shook her head in wonder. "I knew you were smart, but you taking a heartbreaking bit of news, and turning it around in your favor, I'm impressed."

"Thanks, but it won't help until I hear back from Mr. Hunt." Max finally filled his plate, and they ate while making plans for the future.

*****

FIVE DAYS LATER, MAX was out running when his phone rang. For some reason, he hadn't seen Bas since the testing. Something about his parents wanting to take him to see family before he shipped out. Pausing to answer his phone, Max, breathing hard, barked, "Abbott."

"Max?"

"Yes, who's this?" He hadn't looked at the number before answering. Not wanting to cramp, he began walking in circles to keep his heart rate up.

"It's Mr. Hunt. Is there any way you can stop by the school?"

"When?"

"As soon as you can?"

"It'll be a while. I'm running, and I'm seven miles from home. If you don't want a smelly sweaty man in your office, I can be there in two hours."

"That's fine. I'll tell Mrs. Fox you're expected. Come directly to my office."

"Okay, see you soon." Max hung up and moved his head back and forth and went back to running. Since his parents were at work, he ran up the stairs to his room. He showered and changed and ran back down the stairs. He walked into the high school one hour and fifty minutes after hanging up the phone.

Max waved to Mrs. Fox as he strode past the office, and went down the hall to Mr. Hunt's office.

"Max, thanks for coming in. I'll get right to the point. You can't get into the University in Boise until September of next year." Mr. Hunt held up his hand. "However, I can get you into Idaho State University at the Idaho Falls campus this September. You'll have to fill this out and get it back to me no later than Wednesday. Yes, two days from now."

"I'll take it." Max took the packet he was handed, and frowned. "What about financial aid?"

"All the information you need is in that packet. Take it home, fill it out, and get it back to me. I'll try everything in my power to get you in. Luckily, you still have six weeks before fall classes start."

"Thanks, Mr. Hunt." Max rose, shook his hand, and quickly left.

He was elbow deep in paperwork at the dining room table when his best friend walked in. Now was the time to come clean with Bas that he wasn't leaving with him next week.

CHAPTER TEN
SEBASTIAN

"**H**ey, bro!" Bas yelled out as he entered Max's house. He had been gone for the last week and hadn't had the chance to talk to his best friend. He couldn't wait until they left for Parris Island together. It would be so great to go through the Marine boot camp at the same time.

"What's all this." Bas had grabbed the bottle of apple juice from the refrigerator, pulled out a chair, and plopped down. In seconds, half the bottle was gone.

Max drew in a deep breath and held up his hand. "Hold that thought." Then he rifled through the papers and found what he was looking for. Without a word, he passed it to his best friend.

"What's this?"

"Read it?"

Max watched as he did, then braced himself for impact.

"Holy shit, you're not fucking with me?"

"I'm not. I knew the day of the testing. I didn't even get past the first step. Dr. Harris rejected me right then and there. I knew you'd be a few hours, so I went to the library a few blocks away, did some research, then I went back and grabbed your truck and went to the high school."

"Why?"

"I went to talk to Mr. Hunt. Asked if I could get into college. The research I did was for joining the police academy. I need to be twenty-one."

"Shit, so what are you going to do?"

"All this?" Max looked at the papers before him. "This is the application to Idaho State. If I get it back to Hunt by Wednesday. I'll be able to enroll at the Idaho Falls campus in September."

"Damn." Bas jumped to his feet and put his hands in his hair and pulled. He paced in a tight circle and went wider, so he was walking around the whole dining room table.

"Stop," Max said. He looked at his best friend. "I know what you're thinking. Don't. We'll both be okay. You'll join the Marines and be the best you can be. I'll go to college, get a degree, join the police academy, and when the time is right, we'll be together again. Don't give up your dream for my stupidity."

"But I can decline. We can go to school together."

"No," Max said as he rose and went to his friend. "Bas, we can do this. We have e-mail and phones. I know you won't get a lot of time to yourself. If you can, e-mail me when you know you are coming home. I'll make it back here too."

"You're sure?" Bas studied his friend, then chuckled. "Not to sound like a romance novel, but we've been best friends since birth. A few miles and time zones of separation won't hurt that."

"It won't, and if we are true friends, like I believe in my heart, then years from now, we'll have the woman of our dreams between us. That's what I'm looking forward to."

"Yeah," Bas rubbed the back of his neck. "Are you sure you're okay with this?"

"I am. I made the cocky decision to go first. I made you do rock, paper, scissors. This is on me. I do know I'll be able to join the academy, but not until I'm at least twenty-one. Now that Hunt has given me this application, I'm okay with it. I just need you to be okay with my decision."

"It's going to be hard, but I think I can be okay with it, but it's going to be difficult."

The two hugged, then sat down and went over the application line by line. Bas left that night, and Max talked to his parents, but early, even before Max's parents left for work, Bas arrived.

"What the hell?" Max asked, when he felt his covers ripped off him.

"Rise and shine. We only have days left together before life starts. I want to spend as much time with you as I can. I need to store more memories for those lonely nights. Who knows? You never know when I might get sent over to the war."

That was all it took for Max to jump to his feet and dress.

After cooking a big breakfast, they went back to the school and dropped off the application, then spent the next six days inseparable. Max was at Bas's house when a car arrived at four in the morning to take Bas away. It was his Marine recruiter to take him to catch his bus.

After hugging his parents, as well as Max's, Sebastian stood before Max, and said, "No matter what, if we're not together, if you need me for anything, contact me through our first e-mail."

"Same with you. I don't know where I'll end up once I become a police officer. If you get out before me, let me know, and I'll come to you."

"Fair enough." Bas grabbed Max and pulled him into a hug. In his ear, he whispered, "I love you, but not in that way." When Max barked out a laugh, Bas quickly ducked into the waiting car, and didn't look back as he was driven away. He did whisper, "Until we're together again."

THE END

Thank you for taking the time to read this. If you enjoyed this book, please give it some love and leave a review at your preferred site.

You can contact me at:

E-mail: deannalrowley@yahoo.com

Facebook: https://www.facebook.com/Author-Deanna-L-Rowley-106623544172360

Website: https://deannalrowley.com/

Newsletter: https://cheerful-artisan-8318.ck.page/

Goodreads: https://www.goodreads.com/search?q=Deanna+L.+Rowley&qid=1KYE0zxcp5

BookBub: https://www.goodreads.com/search?q=Deanna+L.+Rowley&qid=1KYE0zxcp5

Again, thank you for taking the time to read this.

Please continue reading for other books available for sale and on pre-order.

Also by:

LOVE FOUND SERIES

Love Doesn't Exist: https://books2read.com/u/3GMqA8
Love Is Fleeting: https://books2read.com/u/3JK11P
Love Conquers All: https://books2read.com/u/b5x2Al

SPIES, LIES & RIDES

Aimee's Dilemma: https://books2read.com/u/boEXvp

Hank's Mission: https://books2read.com/u/bQKQew

Colt's Quest: https://books2read.com/u/boEKdp

George's Goal: https://books2read.com/u/bQJ6jD

Hogan's Handful: https://books2read.com/u/47Nx6g

Witt's Warrior's: https://books2read.com/u/mqgV8Z

The rest of the series available for Pre-Order at the following dates:

John's Journey: Pre-Order June 8th: https://books2read.com/u/b6OxnA

Gary's Turn: Pre-Order June 22nd: https://books2read.com/u/4NwZKJ

STORMVILLE – SUSPENSEFUL SEDUCTION WORLD

Samantha A. Cole's Trident Security Books

Bourbon Blaze
https://books2read.com/u/baakP6

Neil's Wish https://books2read.com/u/mZakwl[1]

---

1. https://books2read.com/u/mZakwl

Ginny's Slow Sizzle
https://books2read/u/mowozo

Max and Claire's story continues in the CAPE Investigations Series

Coming in 2021 and available for Pre-Order

Claiming Mia: Available July 6th:

https://books2read.com/u/bwoq6O

Re-Claiming Mia: Available July 13th:

https://books2read.com/u/4jAa85

Protecting Claire: Available Aug. 10th:

https://books2read.com/u/mldYDW

Challenging Claire: Available Aug. 24th:

https://books2read.com/u/mV6QMZ

Taming Sue Ellen: Available Sept. 7th:

https://books2read.com/u/49NWEw

Forgiving Heather: Available Sept. 28th:

https://books2read.com/u/4ERM6g

Defending Melody: Available Oct. 12th:

https://books2read.com/u/3LRGW5

Saving Kate: Available Oct. 26th:
https://books2read.com/u/bzeL0n

Susan Stoker's Universe
Saving Veronica

Lorna's Savior coming July 20th

Elle James' Brotherhood Protection World
Morgan

Coming in 2022
Not Her Series:
Not Her Dom
Not Her Choice
Not Her Rebound
Not Her Problem #1
Not Her Fault
Not Her Problem #2
Not Her Doing
LINKS TO FOLLOW WHEN uploaded for pre-order

ABOUT THE AUTHOR

Deanna has loved to read all her life. She was in the third grade when she fell in love with books while working in the school library. She turned that love of reading into writing. Now Deanna can be found either in her writing cave, sharing her keyboard with her furbaby, reading, or making quilts.

Don't miss out!

Visit the website below and you can sign up to receive emails whenever Deanna L. Rowley publishes a new book. There's no charge and no obligation.

https://books2read.com/r/B-A-WBNL-AMYMB

BOOKS 2 READ

Connecting independent readers to independent writers.